To Barbara

INSIDE IRIS

By

SCOTT GILMORE

Scott Gilmore

For Ollie and Lucie,

My Muse and Inspiration.

CONTENTS

ACKNOWLEDGMENTS

Thank you to the one who shook my hand.

You gave me the push I needed.

To all of my friends and family – your belief and
support are priceless.

CHAPTER 1

Fragmented would be the word I would use to describe Iris when I first met her. Her eyes were like pools of still water that glistened as the clinical white light of the windowless room hit them.

Iris was sitting silently at her metallic steel table in her white pyjama-like clothes, bare footed and concentrating intensely on a puzzle that she must have been given earlier that morning. Iris had a tall, slender build – so much so that the clothes she wore looked like they hung on her. Her pale, porcelain skin was perfect, unblemished, and her near-white hair cascaded down over her shoulders with poker-straight lines. Iris' features were what you could call elven. Her face was fine, her features were small and pointed. The only thing that didn't come across as elven were her perfectly rounded ears that I was sure could hear my heart beat from across the room.

She was real.

The girl sat in front of me was something of a legend, a myth I thought was created by conspiracy theorists the world over. Another spectre of the mysterious government, The Authorities, who controlled everything it was possible to have influence over.

Until that moment, I never believed it. I always had an element of doubt that coursed through my veins but there she was – living, breathing and moving, if only ever so slightly, like a creature doing all it can to preserve energy.

I stood at the door, watching her in silence and in awe. Iris acted as though I wasn't there. I could well have been a ghost in her presence for all the interest she showed in me. Her attention was solely focused on the puzzle on the table in front of her. Iris' hands moved slowly, with an almost smooth, mechanical precision, to move the pieces of shaped wood from one place to the next.

The tray I was carrying into the room became a useless prop that I swiftly slid onto another metallic steel table to my left. The sound of the metallic tray on the table stirred Iris from the task she was focused on and she looked at me through her brow. The irises of her eyes were such bright silver, like mirrors. I felt as though I was being stalked by a big cat, a huntress stalking prey for her young.

"You're new."

I paused and looked at her. It felt like an age before I could find the power to speak as I looked into her silver coloured eyes. "Yes. I'm new."

This reply almost perplexed her and she cocked her head slightly to one side – her gaze uninterrupted. It remained fixed, locked into my eyes. She was not going to let me off that easily.

The tone of Iris' voice was monotonic and smooth, as though she carefully considered every word that was forming in her brain before it entered the world, via her mouth. The words gathered pace and mass, like a snowball rolling down a hill, until they were launched to their intended target.

"You are nervous being here with me."

"Yes, I am. I'm sorry," I apologised, even though I had no reason to. What little confidence I had coming in through the door dissipated, like water vapour from a kettle.

"Are you always this nervous?"

"Sometimes. Normally when I start a new job it can take me a while to find myself." This comment pricked up Iris' interest in me. She saw something in me that was shiny and new – something she wanted to explore.

"Find yourself – that's interesting. If you are not here, where are you?"

When Iris asked me that question, I was speechless. How could I answer? I couldn't answer in any way that would be at all satisfactory, even if I wanted to.

I knew in the short time that I had been talking to her that she was intelligent, and she would see through many if not all answers. It was as though she knew why I was there, that there was something beneath the surface that, if she scratched hard enough in the same place, she could reveal.

"I don't know," I answered, hoping it would be sufficient to satisfy this young girl's curiosity.

"Neither do I," Iris replied with an emotionless expression that saddened and chilled me to the bone at the same time. Iris went back to her task but continued to elaborate. "I have dreams. Not every night but, when I dream, they feel real – so real they have their own smell, taste and sound. It's like I am there.

"People are in my dreams. I can't see their faces. I don't know their names. They are like shadows but warm – like I have a connection with them.

"I'm happy when I'm there. I smile. I laugh. I am a person I have never been before. I like it."

Iris suddenly stopped working at her task, her hand paused millimetres from the puzzle as she thought for a few seconds before looking up at me through her eyebrows. "Then I wake up here and I don't feel. I am this again and the nurses arrive with my medicine and my tasks for the morning."

"Don't you like your tasks?"

"I like them fine but just about fine. They occupy me for long enough until they bring me the next set."

There was little emotion in Iris' face. She continued to speak with her monotonic, frail voice that sounded like it had just about enough life to leave her mouth and fill the air of an area no larger than the room she was in. Why would she need anything more, considering she never left the room?

Iris' hair was just below her shoulders and well brushed – as though the nursing staff who dressed and washed her felt the need to preen her, like a doll in a sterile doll's house. Iris' nails were clipped to a perfect length, her skin washed clean and without a mark on it. Iris was perfect – a doll in her very own prison.

"Do you have anything else to leave for me?"

"No," I replied, "I have nothing else."

"Thank you, I must get on with my tasks."

With that, I turned and left, closing the door behind me, quietly so as not to disturb her. Outside her room stood a medical trolley with a selection of needles and vials with printed labels displaying the name 'Iris'.

It was somewhat disconcerting that so much of this was meant for a girl so young. I'm sure many of the doctors and nurses who walked the corridors before me had the same feelings when they were carrying out the tests and taking samples from a girl who was just fifteen years old and who had been in The Institute since she was a young girl.

As I reached for one of the drawers at the bottom of the trolley, a doctor turned the corner at the bottom of the corridor and made his way towards me. He was in deep conversation with another nurse, an older lady with cold features, making their way purposefully towards Iris' room.

I turned and walked to the elevator beside me and

hit the button to go down. The noise of the nurse's and doctor's footsteps got louder as they approached me from down the corridor.

The conversation they were having also came into focus. They were discussing how the samples they were to take had to get to the lab for tests immediately.

The digits above the door changed, ascending to the floor I was on. I knew the elevator was fast, but to me, in those moments, the digits moved in slow motion. Beads of sweat started to gather and run slowly down my back. With every bead of sweat that gathered, by heart started to beat harder.

The elevator bell finally dinged, and the door opened. I entered as smoothly and calmly as I could, trying not to draw attention to myself, and pressed the button for the ground floor. As the door slowly closed, the voices neared. Suddenly I heard the nurse. "I swore I set the tray of food on the trolley."

The door closed, and the lift descended.

CHAPTER 2

The windows of the train were a silent barrier between me and the outside world. Multiple shades of green merged with browns as bushes blended with trees and hedges. The continuous stream of colour transfixed me. I had not slept in over twenty-four hours and sleep was slowly catching up on me. My mind was misfiring, kicking in and sputtering to an unsatisfactory conclusion.

Every so often, my eyes felt heavy and they would close momentarily, even for a few minutes, and I would waken with a start. Each time my eyes closed, a slightly different scenario that had its roots in what happened earlier on that day would play in my mind. In one, the doctor and nurse recognised I wasn't supposed to be there and caught me. In another, Iris got spooked by me being a strange face and called for help. Finally, in the last one I approached Iris when I entered her room and she didn't move. When I got beside her I whispered her name and touched her shoulder, only for her to shatter into thousands of pieces at my feet.

With all of these odd mini-dreams that played in my overheated, hyperactive brain, I knew I had to sleep ahead of my meeting. The others would be expecting answers and even though I didn't have many, what I did have I would have to relay back to them.

The distant, almost incoherent hum of the train engine as it pulled the carriages through the winding hills of the countryside was as calming to me as a heartbeat in the womb. Every so often, the train would lurch slightly left or right as it turned on the tracks and this would rock me even further into sleep.

Half past twelve, I thought as I looked at my watch and yawned. The timetable at the station said the train would arrive in Hexingham West at one-forty-five. I knew I could get at least an hour's sleep before waking to gather myself and fight through the bustling crowds at the station while, at the same time, trying to remain fully calm and dodge the looks of any Security Forces, who were always on duty at the station.

My cold, half-finished cup of coffee sat on the table in front of me, but I couldn't stomach it with the worry of whether the nurse had figured out that *I* had taken the tray into Iris' room or if Iris mentioned that a new nurse brought her the food and described me to her.

I half expected to be met by the Security Forces when the train pulled up and carted off to prison. As the coffee was all I had to drink, I got up from my cabin and went to the dining car to get some water and use the toilet.

The train was full for a Wednesday afternoon. The cabins were all occupied with businessmen and other professionals typing and swiping away on their tablet screens. Tens of people, like zombies, staring. Their eyes scanning over words, pictures and documents, each with their own importance and deadlines to be read or written.

The door to the dining car hissed open smoothly and the clatter and noise of food and drink being served ruined the near silence of my carriage. The smell of coffee and prepacked foods from all over the world filled the air, like perfume. If I didn't feel ill with worry that I had been discovered at The Institute, I would probably have made the choice much earlier to get some food. It was lunch time after all and I knew I had a long day ahead of me.

I ordered some snacks and a bottle of purified water. I made my way back to my cabin and locked the door, being sure to check I hadn't been followed from the dining car.

The bottle of water was ice cold and gradually numbed my fingers and hand the longer I held it. Years ago, people used to be able to drink water from taps and drink bottled water as a choice. I was one of millions of people in the country who didn't have that choice. It was either drink the purified water or get sick.

Many years before I was born, the government allowed people to drill for fuels in the ground. People protested that they didn't want these companies to be doing this because, during the process, they had to use chemicals that could be poisonous if they were to get mixed up with drinking water as it passed through the land.

When these protests were brought to the Prime Minister at the time, he 'considered' them but in the end allowed the companies to drill.

Things were fine for a while but eventually people started to get sick. It wasn't long before the protestors heard of this and demanded the government did something to punish these companies and the people in charge of them for not fully revealing the dangers of the chemicals used and their impact on the environment.

In the end, the drinking water was contaminated and couldn't be drank without using purification tablets or drinking bottled or canned drinks. The purified water didn't taste bad, it just tasted a little different, but my grandmother could never drink it. "Disgusting," she would say. "Give me water out of the tap any day."

I took out my phone and checked the message I received from Carl before I boarded the train.

I can't believe it is really her! If what you said is true, this will bring it all down. 6pm @ Bethlehem. C X

I just wanted to get back home and to safety. Even though I was in my own cabin and locked the door, I felt exposed. There was no doubt that if the nurse suspected me at The Institute, I would be on their radar and Iris would most likely be moved to another facility – lost forever.

I listened back to the words Iris spoke in the room. Her recorded voice was haunting, like it was a hollow shell. A girl was in there – a real girl with a personality, hopes, dreams and fears. The more I played back the recording, the more emotional I got.

When I look back at those feelings, those emotions that started to well up inside me, I found it odd that I felt so strongly for the welfare of a girl that I had only met once in person. Her life was one of myth among The Resistance and I had read so much about her and what had apparently happened in her young life. Her story was one that intrigued me and through reading about her, I felt close to her, like I was gazing through a looking glass and seeing her live, move and breathe.

After spending two years tracking Iris down, I had already become attached to the idea of her but, now I had found her, the attachment became all the more real. *'I'm happy when I'm there. I smile. I laugh. I am a person I have never been before. I like it,'* were the words that I kept scanning back to listen to over and over.

These were not the words of a teenage girl. These were the words of a prisoner, a captive in an environment that was not one that they were naturally supposed to be in.

Years ago, when people used to keep animals in zoos, certain people believed that was disgusting and animals deserved to be in the wild. In the end, that's what led to zoos being outlawed except for seriously endangered animals so scientists could try to find a way to increase their numbers and release more into the wild at a later date.

For years, there were protests against zoos. People of all ages felt so strongly that the treatment of animals in these places was disgraceful that they protested up and down the country, calling for the animals to be returned to their native environment.

Eventually, The Authorities gave in and started to export the animals to other countries and then close down the zoos. The voice of the people had won, and everything returned to normal.

As I listened over and over again to Iris' voice on my phone, I asked myself what would happen if Iris' story got out and people knew how she was being treated inside the walls of The Institute. Would the same animal rights activists turn their attention to Iris and use their voices in the same vitriolic tone to free her, or would The Authorities simply tell them that it was necessary and crack down on anyone who refused to walk away and back down?

It was impossible to tell.

Iris was a young girl who should have been out in the real world, living, growing, learning about what it was to be a teenager, making mistakes and learning by them. Instead, she was a lab rat, a person who had something of use to The Authorities and they wanted to extract it – to mine it and use it for whatever ends they had planned for it.

The more I researched Iris, the more it dawned on me that there was no way she could have been the only person who The Authorities and The Institute could have experimented on. Even then, for all we knew, they could have had ten Irises all working to the same goal, whatever it may be.

Being from a journalistic background, I knew there were always two sides to every story and that there would be some shady uses for the subjects, like Iris, but I also knew there *had* to be some other tests that were being carried out too. When I looked at the world through my trained eyes, I started to see it through a series of filters that would bend and tint the light to help me get a clearer picture.

To me, all of the theories and stories I had heard through my time with The Resistance helped add another filter to my mind's eye. I believed a lot of what they told me and what I had researched while with them, but I also knew that they had their own agenda, just like The Authorities did.

I just had to see what I needed to in the full spectrum of colour that was opening up before me.

Soon enough, the voice called out over the intercom, 'Good afternoon, citizens, we have arrived in Hexingham West. The time is now one-forty-three p.m. Please disembark the train carefully and ensure you have all of your belongings. Any belongings that are left behind will be treated as suspicious and incinerated. Thank you for travelling with us this afternoon. Have a nice day.'

I did as the announcer asked and made my way through the carriage and out of the door onto the platform. The near deafening quiet of the carriage gave way to an equally deafening roar of a busy train station in the middle of the afternoon.

The platforms were alive with commuters, teeming from one train to the next. Many of the commuters, with earpieces in, talked in an indecipherable chatter while scanning miniscule information on the lenses of their eyewear. No one paid attention to where they were or whom they may run into. Their life and their reality was contained within one ear and one eye as actual reality happened all around them.

A truly one-dimensional view.

The sweet smell of recycled air was almost sickly as it wafted through the bodies of commuters and stationary trains. Even though it made me feel ill at times, I would much rather breathe in the recycled air than the air I breathed in when I was younger.

The acrid, bitter taste of exhaust fumes through a cloth facemask was much more sickening. I remembered the taste clearly, even though fossil fuels had been banned for ten years or more. It was a taste that was hard to forget and one that the governments all over the world took seriously to remove when they installed the recycling units. The Authorities in Britain made it their priority and swift action was taken. From the North of Scotland to the South of England, the smoking chimneys of factories and power stations ceased pumping out their fumes and the new, cleaner Equinox reactors came online, powering the nation's towns and cities all across the country.

Huge circular structures were dotted around the skylines of every major city to filter and recycle the air as it blew through the space in the centre. The citizens felt angry at having to pay the extra taxes to build them at the time but everyone started to see the benefits almost immediately – one of the few benefits the governments around the world declared was for the 'greater good'.

Outside the station, I found a taxi to take me to Bethlehem – the name of our sanctuary.

CHAPTER 3

I paid the driver and waited until he pulled away from the kerb before I walked off. I knew I was being paranoid but, at the time, I felt it was better to be safe than sorry. The stories we had heard and researched about fellow activists being followed, harassed, beaten or even killed for 'stirring things up' made us all paranoid. Even regular citizens who weren't interested in investigating wrongs or trying to find out truths were terrified of being pointed out by others as inciting disorder.

The government really had all citizens under fear of doing wrong and it was clear when we tried to talk to witnesses or sources that were passed on to us.

Few spoke and, those who did, went into and stayed in hiding – who could blame them? When you lived in a world that resembled Salem at the height of the Witch Trials, you would prefer to keep your head below the parapet to save it being shot off – or being burned at the stake for a belief or a view that had never even entered your mind.

The streets hummed with people weaving in and out of cafés, shops and generally making their way from place to place. Cars passed seamlessly at a constant steady speed with passengers working, reading or talking as the vehicles made their way to a pre-programmed destination.

Every so often, the flow of traffic stopped simultaneously for pedestrians to cross – simply walking out into the road, safe in the knowledge that the computers wouldn't allow the cars to hit them with the thousands of cameras and sensors dotted around every street corner to detect if something living was to be hit by something that was not when moving at speed.

Bethlehem was no more than a five-minute walk from where I got out of the taxi. I kept my head down and listened to some classical music. Classical music always calmed me. It gave me a few minutes away from the chaos around me, blocking out all noise and tumult that would undoubtedly cause my anxiety to rise.

As I made my way through the busy pedestrian traffic, everything appeared to slow as the string section slowly meandered through its piece. Cars slowed down, the hum and chatter of people's voices melted away until all I could hear was music.

Across the street, a group of people were arguing over something, their hands waving up and down, almost conducting the orchestra in my head.

Behind them, the Security Forces, in their red uniforms, vests and red berets, strolled up slowly to no doubt 'diffuse the situation' in no time through their mere presence. If required, I was sure they would be able to suppress any violence or disturbances using their usual weapon of choice – a stun gun to the lower back before trailing the culprits away to a cell for the evening ahead of a speedy trial the next morning.

I turned left, down an alleyway, and stopped at the steel door. I took out my phone and sent a message, *I'm here.* Inside a matter of seconds, the door slid open and I stepped into Bethlehem.

Carl greeted me with a hug and I buried my head into his chest, throwing my arms around him. Still with my music playing, he spoke something to me simply because I felt the vibrations in his throat and chest. I didn't care what he said, all I cared about was the feeling that I was safe.

I felt like Beethoven; feeling the change in frequency as Carl's voice went up and down in pitch and grew louder and softer comforted me more than I thought it would.

I turned off my music and put away my headphones. Carl's smile told me he was as relieved to see me as I was him. I didn't need to hear what he said, he was glad I made it back.

"Seth wants to see you," Carl said in a serious tone. I knew Carl was unhappy that Seth suggested I was the one to go to The Institute and, from his tone, I knew he still felt angry about it.

Something about Carl's caring about my safety flattered me but I also felt frustrated and tired of sitting in the background while others took ownership of their own little piece of the struggle. No matter how much Carl protected me and wanted to keep me away from the realities that we all faced, I needed to see it. Just hearing second-hand testimonies of what was happening wasn't enough now. I needed to get my hands dirty and if that meant bruising Carl's manliness and ego then so be it.

Suddenly, the relief and comfort I felt when arriving

at Bethlehem was stripped away and the old, common feelings I had before I left on the mission to The Institute resurfaced. Gritting my teeth and breathing in a deep, calming breath, I walked off, leaving Carl stood on the same spot on which he greeted me.

I made my way up to see Seth. Seth had never doubted me from the minute I set foot into Bethlehem for the first time. I remember when he greeted me and shook my hand, he stared into my eyes with an intensity that burned right through me.

His hazel eyes were piercing, making you almost powerless to move away unless he wanted you to go. His long, brown hair was almost always tied up into a bun at the back of his head and his short beard gave him an identity similar to one of the most famous revolutionaries in history, Che Guevara.

The first night I attended The Resistance, he sat us all down, and asked us each what it was that made us want to join the struggle. Some people had very deep, heart-breaking stories of people they cared about being abducted, beaten and even murdered. Others had a general curiosity that was extinguished as soon as it flickered into existence, like a candle in the draught of an open door. These people never returned. They had taken a look at what was on offer and what was expected of them. To return to their simple, monotonous life in the world provided for them by The Authorities was the easier road to take.

I never liked to follow the roads travelled by others. Even when I was a little girl, when my parents took me to forests and parks, I would often trail off into what felt like the wilderness for a little girl of eight or nine years old.

The bright sunlight would be stripped away by the canopy of the trees above, the silence of my footsteps on the soft grass would give way the crunches and snaps of dead leaves and twigs underfoot.

My parents would call me, but they would rarely, if ever, panic because I slipped away so often. Their voices would linger in the distance, keeping me safe and secure in the knowledge that they were not far away, but they were far away enough for me to feel like I was free. I was away from the noise and bedlam of modern-day life. I was a child of the forest, opening my senses, my eyes, ears and nose to the environment that enveloped me. For those moments, life was special, life was freedom.

Life was mine.

My story began with Carl. Without him, I would never have heard about The Resistance. For the first six months I worked at *The Tribune*, we were on the same breaks and naturally started talking.

It wasn't long before Carl started sharing his anger at having to change stories and testimonies from sources on orders from our editors. The more he pushed to write 'the truth', the more disgruntled he got and then left after a blazing row with the editors. As he walked out carrying his few belongings from his desk, he gave me a salute and a smile.

Two months later, I was in a café reading a book when Carl sat down opposite me with the same book. "Snap!" he said, making me jump and half smile in the process. I don't know what it was about him that intrigued me so much.

Carl rarely shaved, and his face was usually covered in a reddish-brown stubble that was slightly redder than the messy, unbrushed hair that sat on top of his head. He was tall, the first thing I noticed about him when we met as he towered head and shoulders above me.

Outside *The Tribune*, he wore scruffy, plain clothes that made him look totally different from the guy who wore V-neck jumpers and suit trousers every day, no matter how hot it was. Carl's wrinkled jeans, beaten up white trainers and khaki green T-shirt made him look decidedly normal which, with hindsight, was his choice. It ensured he 'blended in with the plebs', in his own words.

Normally, I would have said that he wasn't my type, but I knew there was something about him that I was unable to take my eyes and thoughts from. He had a rogue's smile and didn't care what anyone thought about him.

His explosion at the editor and his salute at me as he left that day made me feel that there was a substance to Carl that I had never come across before in any man up until then. So many men were self-obsessed narcissists who saw themselves as a one-man springboard to boost society. They weren't. I was able to see through them in no time and I got bored. As I saw it, before I met Carl, I much preferred my own company than that of others.

Others bored me.

That day, Carl and I got talking and exchanged numbers. We dated soon after that and, before long, he introduced me to Bethlehem and Seth. I think, when Carl first brought me to Bethlehem, he wanted me to see him in his element, writing and contributing to their online publication but, in the time since he'd left *The Tribune*, I had met sources who had opened my eyes to many truths I had never believed before. At Bethlehem, I started to see a jealous, almost controlling side to Carl I'd never seen before.

I was never the type of person to sit behind a man and watch him impress me. I was never a cheerleader who got weak at the knees when a man put on a show for me. I needed more. I needed something for me and, as these desires started to surface, Carl started to change towards me and I didn't like that.

He'd turned my head to look at the truth but now, when he tried to turn my head away, I wanted to see more. I wanted to bathe in it. I wanted it to envelop me and I didn't care what effect it had on me. I didn't care if I was arrested. I wanted to be a part of it and if I were to be swept away in the tide then so be it.

I sat, that first night in Bethlehem, and shared my reasons for being there and had everyone, including Seth, engrossed in every word I said. For the first time, I held the room. People were interested in me and what I had to say.

I told them about some of the stories I'd had to rewrite because my editors said so. I told them about the sources that were silenced. I told them about the emotional stories people shared with me, about how they cried and begged me to help find their missing relatives. People who were there one day and then gone the next.

The room was silent. I could barely hear a breath, never mind anyone else trying to cut in on what I was saying or add to the points I was making. The floor was mine and I was dancing. The lights were focused on me and the audience were captivated as I glided, spun and posed my way to the movements of the music.

They were eating out of the palm of my hand.

Seth didn't take his eyes off me once as I shared my reasons for being there that night. His eyes were pinned to me and, in the dull light of the room we were in, it was as though his eyes were two black holes, pulling me into him and his cause, his beliefs, his struggle.

After I spoke, Seth stood up and spoke to us all. "You have all come here for different reasons tonight and I know it was not easy for any of you to walk through that door and into our world. Some of you may not decide to become actively involved, some of you may return and be as integral to The Resistance as I am myself.

"The struggle we face every single day is real. Outside these walls people are being abducted, people are being oppressed and our beliefs and freedoms as a civilised society are under threat. I fear that, if we sit here and do nothing, the world that we knew will be gone forever and we will be truly lost."

I was enthralled. When the others left, Seth came to me and was taken by the stories I had shared with the group. Being a forty-something who had obviously experienced much more than I had in The Resistance, I waited to speak with him but felt sick with nerves. I had entered a world that was alien to me and Carl was not there to direct me.

"Jade, isn't it?" he asked.

"Yes." I shook his hand, which he shook but also cupped with a second hand. "Thank you for welcoming me tonight."

"It was a pleasure. Your stories really hit home with the group tonight, thank you for sharing." I was about to say, *don't mention it,* or, *no problem,* but Seth got in ahead of me. "One story really got my attention and I wondered if you would sit with me a little longer and tell me everything you know."

"Um, sure, which story was it?"

Seth's look changed from welcoming warmth to a steely seriousness that I had not seen earlier that evening. "The young girl at The Institute."

CHAPTER 4

Seth was sat silently at his desk with his tablet computer. He didn't lift his head or even acknowledge me as I entered the room. The expression he wore on his face was long, worn and tired, as though he had been waiting what felt like an age for me to arrive with positive news.

Only when the door closed, did Seth recognise that I had arrived. He smiled. "Your transcript and recording is…"

"You like it? I wasn't sure if…"

The repeated interrupting was a sign that we were both bundles of nerves. He was nervous in case I was caught and captured. I was nervous in case I was caught and captured too. With this collective sharing of anxiety, the interrupting was reassuring to me to know that Seth was relieved to see me as much as read and hear Iris' voice.

"It's perfect. It is everything we could ever have hoped for." I paused, waiting for him to continue. Seth looked up. "She's real, Jade. It's really her!"

"It is her. It's Iris."

As I looked at Seth, I knew he was emotional. It was as though he was holding back emotions that he hadn't experienced in a long time. The dormant emotions were resurfacing, and I felt as though he was in the middle of trying to comprehend what he was feeling as I entered the room.

Suddenly, the forty-something who I looked up to, appeared to be that much more fragile. I knew that he played a part for the rest of us at times, but this was the first time any one of us had seen him show even the slightest moment of weakness.

Goliath had become David.

"I have been waiting for this moment for a long time, I'm sorry," he said, softly. Seth sat up, set the tablet computer down and composed himself as he leant forward to address me.

"I understand. We've all been hoping for this day for a long time now."

On Seth's tablet, he had a grainy picture that a

website claimed was Iris. I knew it wasn't her, but I didn't say anything. "Take a seat, we have a lot to discuss." Seth saw me look at the tablet and slid it into his bag. I felt that although he was determined to find and free Iris for his own agenda, she had become his obsession in the months leading up to my mission to The Institute. "How is Carl after our... discussion last time we were together?"

"He's fine with it," I lied.

"Good, because we have so much more we need to do now that we know the truth. Iris is just the tip of the iceberg. Beneath her are many layers that we haven't even begun to explore yet.

"She is our priority from now on in. I want everyone to take what you have found and focus all our attentions on getting her out."

I paused, almost in disbelief at what he was planning to do. "You want to...? How?"

"Before you joined us here, we had some plans to break into The Institute for another mission but now we have Iris, we will adapt them to get her out instead."

I knew that my face gave away the fact that I was shocked to learn that Seth wanted us to move that quickly. Trying to hide it was pointless and I think Seth knew that I would react that way, which was why he didn't react at all. "You do realise how difficult…"

"I do but it has to be done."

With the amount of times Seth was interrupting me, I knew he was determined but I also knew there was something else he wasn't telling me. "What is it about Iris?"

"How do you mean?"

"Ever since we first met, you wanted to hear about her, you asked me to go over what I found out multiple times. I don't mean to be out of line but, if we are to risk our freedom, lives and possibly Iris' life, we need to know everything."

Seth paused and looked away for a second before taking a deep breath and sighing. He opened his mouth as though he was going to say something, but instead he paused and looked away again. I felt like I wanted to press him to find out what it was he was going to say, but I knew when to press and when to let things go.

My journalistic experience had at least taught me that. A good lead was like a butterfly, you could hold it in the palm of your hand and it may interact with you but, with the slightest movement, you could spook it and all that delicate beauty could flutter away into the wind.

When researching the story of the missing girl, I found out that the girl's parents were also activists but on a minor level. They were part of a different, more moderate group who took their daughter to a local facility for the compulsory 'tests' to check for diseases, genetic deformities and also genetic 'gifts' that could be of use to further advance society.

The tests were compulsory for all children between the age of three and four and were pre-arranged. If parents refused to bring their children to the tests, they could be arrested, jailed and even have their children removed from them and rehoused with more willing families.

The story was that the parents took their daughter to the tests and, once they found that she tested positive for possessing 'desirable qualities', they refused to let their daughter have more invasive testing. Apparently, on their way home, the parents were stopped by the Security Forces, the girl was forcibly taken, and the parents were never seen again.

When the family asked the Security Forces to investigate, they were palmed off with excuses and nothing ever seemed to move on. The parents of the disappeared would turn up faithfully every week for months to find out if there was any development in the case only to be told that there was nothing.

A year or so later, they claimed they found the 'suspect' who had killed the whole family and buried them somewhere in a nearby forest.

The family never believed the Security Forces' story but then the suspect was found unconscious in prison ahead of his trial. While being treated in the prison infirmary, the suspect never woke, and his life support machine was switched off. The investigators were unable to find out where the bodies were buried.

The whole story didn't make sense but that was the story The Authorities stuck to and remained the only explanation for what happened until rumours surfaced of a young girl, the same age as the girl who disappeared, who was in a medical facility called The Institute.

The poor families continued to turn up at their local Security Station and ask if any progress had been made, repeating their belief that there *had* to be another explanation. Time and time again they were told the same thing and sent on their way.

This pattern continued until the grandparents of the disappeared girl gradually died. Five years after she disappeared, her last surviving grandmother passed away in her sleep. She died still asking for her son and her granddaughter.

As soon as I shared the story about the disappearance with Seth, he took a real interest in me and Carl didn't like it. When Seth asked me to go to The Institute and pose as a nurse, I was excited but also worried because I had never done anything like this before. Any other tasks I had been assigned were all general propaganda-based jobs or helping the digital team with their online duties and opening up about the truth of the stories I was made to change by my editor – under an alias of course.

The more I got involved with The Resistance, I felt disgusted by the work I was doing at *The Tribune* and spoke to Seth about resigning. During one of our discussions about Iris, Seth said it was important that I remained at the newspaper because it gave me a great cover to investigate and, even if I did have to change the stories, I could use my alias with The Resistance to write the true story.

This appeased me enough to carry on with my work at the newspaper and Seth was right. I was able to interview people, talk to sources and investigate disappearances but all under the umbrella of *The Tribune* as an official journalist.

The Authorities didn't seem to mind journalists

appearing to do their job honestly and with apparent dedication. All they needed to do was put editors in charge of the newspapers who would force the journalists under them to change the stories to a positive light. The people would see the stories being written about and, as the press still came across as having some shreds of dignity in the eyes of the people, The Authorities felt they helped calm people by proving the stories were all false and 'made up in the overactive imaginations of trouble makers who just wanted to see our world burn'.

A perfect cover.

The Authorities would play the game themselves when ousting people who they felt had been too vocal or who fell out of favour with the regime. The editors would have stories fed to them about corruption or immorality committed by members of the government and pass them on to us to investigate.

When we investigated the stories, and found dirt on the subjects of our stories, the articles were rarely changed and, before long, the subject would be ousted in disgrace. Usually, something unfortunate would happen to the disgraced former politicians and the dirt they left with would die with them.

Seth thanked me again for the work I had done. It

was 'invaluable', he said, and we would get to planning the mission to get Iris out of The Institute the next day. We were all exhausted, whether it be me, going through with the mission itself, or people at Bethlehem, worrying about whether I would make it or be captured and cave in during interrogation to lead The Authorities right to Seth, Carl and the others.

I left all my recordings with Seth, hugged him and left to find Carl. I had a feeling that my being reunited with Carl was going to be a little awkward.

CHAPTER 5

"He's pleased then," Carl asked as he swung back on his chair, leaning against the wall behind him.

"Of course."

"Good." Carl sipped at his coffee and cupped the mug in two hands. He stared into the steam almost looking for something to talk about instead of what he really wanted to discuss with me. It was as though he was looking for words to string together out of the twisting, turning water vapor that rose from the mouth of the mug.

I sipped on my coffee but, instead of peering into my mug, I looked through the rising steam to see what Carl was doing, how he was fidgeting and if he was going to speak next or I.

He always did this. He was someone who couldn't keep still when there was something on his mind. It was annoying when all I wanted was for him to spit it out but, on the other hand, it was easy to see when something irked him. He was a jitterbug, almost vibrating before he finally opened up enough to let whatever was annoying him out – like a caged animal bolting from captivity when the door of the cage was left open.

"Aren't you glad to see me?" I asked, frustrated with the silence. Something which Carl knew and always preyed upon when we had just had an argument.

Carl looked up at me. The look in his eyes was one of resignation. He knew that I was aware that something was bothering him. "Why wouldn't I be?"

"Because you're looking more longingly at that cup of coffee than you are at me." I paused for a few seconds before approaching the subject I really wanted to discuss. To open up the little box that could lead to a huge row, but I was unable to resist. "I at least thought that you'd apologise."

Those were the words that pricked his attention and he looked up, his eyes snapping instantaneously from the coffee into mine. "Why?" he snapped. His tone was sharp. His word, that single, solitary word, cut me.

"Do you really need me to remind you?"

Carl looked away into the corner of the room. Avoidance was how he always chose to deal with things that upset him or moments when he was in the wrong and refused to own up. "I just don't know what to say."

"Start with 'sorry' and we can go from there."

Carl looked back at me and held my gaze for a long time. In his eyes I knew he was sorry for what had happened, but I needed him to say it – he couldn't. "Fine," I said as I got up and poured the remnants of my coffee down the drain, with a force that accidentally spattered the white tiles on the wall behind the sink with dark brown specks.

"I don't see why I should be the only one to apologise, Jade," he said sharply, getting up from his seat and walking purposefully towards me. "I mean you…"

I turned fiercely. "I what?! What *exactly* did I do?"

Carl couldn't answer. Inside, I knew he didn't believe what the chemicals, emotions and suspicion in his mind wanted him to see, to visualise and obsess about. Carl rarely could ever let things go. Even when the issue was dead and buried, he would always look for the metaphorical shovel to dig it back up again.

"You want me to apologise for something that I *did not do*. You want me to open myself up and beg forgiveness for something that is buried deep down in some dark place inside that paranoid head of yours, but I won't, Carl."

Carl stood, motionless, expecting me to say something that he felt had been coming for a while before. At times, yelling at Carl was like yelling at a puppy dog. He would look at you with those big, brown eyes and tug at every heartstring he could to get a tune out of you to forgive him, but this time it didn't work.

This time, I knew he was in the wrong.

"I'm going to go home, get a shower and go to bed. I suggest you do the same and then tomorrow you can go find someone else who's willing to put up with whatever *this* is because I'm done." I walked straight out of the canteen and out into the rainy, night-time streets.

As I descended the stairs and let the door close with a sharp, metallic thud behind me, I didn't once think about Carl. All I could think about was the fact that what The Resistance were doing about Iris was much more important than the petty games Carl wanted to play. I was in no place to deal with his

42

issues and his controlling nature.

I had to think and think with clarity.

I had to be free to focus on whatever Seth and the others had planned out for me.

The streets were still busy. It was nine in the evening and cars swished by on the damp street. The rain poured so heavily that each drop landed with a clap and almost bounced back to where it came from, but I didn't care. Each drop that fell on me washed me of all my worries, stresses and anger.

The gradual cold dampness that was seeping through my clothes was cathartic, like I was being cleansed of all that was bothering me. My mind started to take wings and fly free.

When I was a girl, I used to walk in the rain regularly when my parents were fighting. They would start into one another about petty nonsense and I would just get my coat, my music and go. When I left, they never came after me. I would walk the streets listening to various playlists I made, not making eye contact with people just in case they recognised me and asked if I was ok.

The world could have stopped for all I knew back then. Everyone could have frozen and I would not have noticed or batted an eyelid at the change. I would walk around and see people living their lives as though they hadn't the slightest care in the world. They would walk, almost in slow motion, laughing and teasing one another or simply just *living*. In those days, I was just about existing.

I was embarrassed.

I was ashamed of myself for letting them affect me the way they did.

What would I say to them? Would I lie? How would I lie? What would I say? Would they believe me? Would they call the police to bring me back? Would they notice I cried? Would they care?

All of these questions were in my mind as I walked those night. As a girl, I knew the rain would hide the tears. As I grew up, I just accepted my parents' fights as normality.

As an adult, walking through the dark, near-flooded streets, I *did* have questions metamorphizing in my mind from answers I had given before, like a butterfly, which was once a caterpillar, hatching from a chrysalis. I knew that life was meant to test me, and I had to let my issues wash over me, like the rain that fell that evening. The difference was that, being older and having more life experience, I was able to answer some of the queries my mind threw at me. There were more complex questions that burned inside me, like a branding iron leaving a mark, that could not be answered right away – would we get Iris out of The Institute, what was Seth's *real* agenda with Iris and, once she was out of her captivity inside the research centre, what would become of her?

I passed takeaway restaurants that were serving people drunk and others taking shelter from the weather. They all looked at me and leant in, obviously talking about me as I passed but thankfully my music drowned out the rain as well as their words. Their words that judged me, labelled me and viewed me as a lesser person in their eyes.

The whole way down the street, neon lights from various shops and restaurants reflected on the soaking wet ground. The reflections danced and shimmered in the rippling water as the raindrops pounded the pavement below. The lights merged into a kaleidoscope of colour on the floor and the little girl in me felt like she was walking on a rainbow as she made her way through the dark night.

As I walked, I thought about Iris in that room with no windows. I imagined her lying there, staring up at the ceiling, not asleep but not awake. Her silver eyes almost glistening in whatever dull light shone in through the viewing panel in the door and the slit from beneath it.

Was she thinking about me? Did she know I was not one of the nurses? Was she upset? Did she feel *anything*?

I heard her voice, the words she spoke to me, and I wanted to go back to when I was stood there holding that tray. I wanted to talk to her. I wanted to ask her questions. I wanted to do something more than what I did – nothing.

Immediately, I felt regret burn in my stomach. That was my chance to talk to her. I knew so much about her life and what others said happened to her and all I wanted to do was question her about what *she* knew and what *she* remembered when she was young – straight from the horse's mouth.

I then heard Carl's voice. The words he said to me. The way he spoke to me. How he didn't believe in me. All of the thoughts I was having about Iris were washed away and replaced by my anger that he wouldn't believe me. He would believe those paranoid voices in his head and what some others within The Resistance were telling him rather than the words of the person he apparently loved.

I was not the kind of girl who believed in happily

ever afters or love at first sight. I was always sceptical of relationships, love and marriage but one thing I never backed down on was the truth. When that truth involved me and the person I was trying to convince didn't believe me, I was desperate to prove my innocence – to prove that they were wrong, and I was right.

That was why I believed so strongly in working for *The Tribune* and fighting to unearth truths for people who had been wronged, lied to and whose lives had been destroyed by those in positions of power.

Soon enough, I got home and closed the door behind me.

My apartment was small but was all I needed and wanted. When I left for college, all I wanted was a place away from people and my parents and this place was perfect.

My living area was attached to the kitchen, which was small but functional, and divided by a breakfast bar. The kitchen was clean, simply because I knew I had to prepare food there and, if I let it get into a state, I would most likely get ill and I hated being sick. This was where I made my first stop to make a coffee to replace the one I couldn't stomach finishing in Bethlehem with Carl.

I went straight into my bedroom. All around the room were scattered clothes of varying levels of cleanness as well as some papers from stories passed to me by my editor.

I got out of my soaking clothes and into the shower. The water felt scorching hot against my freezing cold skin, but it felt amazing. I stood leaning against the wall of the shower, letting the water run over me. The cold water washed away my worries and pains. The hot water healed me.

I was reborn.

Eventually I got washed, dried, dressed and collapsed into bed. I lay there staring at the ceiling, totally disinterested in sleep.

Outside, sirens blared, and the flashing blue lights lit up the darkness outside my window. The rain hammered hard on the window and my neighbour's TV could be heard faintly, like a friend keeping me company in the distance. I listened to the voices for what felt like hours with my eyes closed, resting them hoping that eventually my mind would give in and sleep.

Eventually, it did.

CHAPTER 6

I woke the next morning with the drone of the alarm radio playing from across the room. I thought putting it there would make me get out of bed to switch it off but, after the day and night I had the day before, I just wished I had chosen to put it within arm's reach to turn it off.

The whole time I lay in the bed, listening to the presenters talk of news and current affairs, I hoped not to hear of an intruder at The Institute, but they never mentioned anything about it.

The night before, as I was drifting off to sleep, I couldn't help but play a plethora of scenarios in my head showing various ways that I would be captured. Some of them involved me being taken peacefully in the street on my way to *The Tribune*. Others involved the Security Forces breaking down the door at

Bethlehem or of my apartment and stunning me with their stun gun as I lay flopping uncontrollably on the floor, like a fish out of water.

All of the talk was of new initiatives to bring in new laws to limit the travel of people with HX7 – a relatively new illness that people were beginning to develop across parts of Eastern Europe, in countries like Romania and Bulgaria.

"Outbreaks of the flu-like virus have been detected in the easternmost parts of Europe," reported the journalist on the morning news. "In Bucharest, a centre has been set up to treat those affected but the Romanian Health Minister, Nicolae Pruteanu, has assured the public that the government is doing everything in its power to treat its people and find an answer to this latest health problem."

The journalist spoke about plans to bring a select group of the people suffering with the illness into a medical facility in the Shetland Islands, on the Isle of Bressay, to research it in more detail. This research centre was where The Authorities researched the more dangerous diseases. The Resistance had come to the conclusion that the area was chosen because it was so remote, and it would be easy to cover up any mistakes that were made or problems that arose from the research.

Of course, the rounding up of people with HX7 didn't seem to anger or annoy anyone as the majority of the population in countries across Europe wanted nothing more than to find a cure for any illnesses that started to infect the population, full stop. If people were experimented on, so what? If people were subjected to what was pretty much torture, so what? If people died, so what?

The minds of the moral and just can swiftly turn into something resembling Dr Frankenstein if they felt the greater good was worth the sacrifice. The hearts of the nation were turned from hearts of gold into hearts of darkness, viewing any 'advance' in research as a gift from God and it was not to be questioned. Unless, you were a relative of one the victims – then, you wanted answers, but you had no one to question and had no idea what questions to ask.

Many people across the world were growing increasingly anxious about the development of new illnesses and diseases that were threatening the way we went about life on a daily basis. Some of the illnesses were contagious and others were debilitating to people and caused them to stop working or, in the worst cases, have to rely on care in new hospitals that governments started to build in the countryside, away from the main population in the cities.

The outbreaks of illnesses caused a huge wave of paranoia to sweep the population, almost like a virus in itself. No one knew who was ill and, if they were ill, were they contagious? Could they infect everyone else just by being in contact with them?

In some cases, groups of vigilantes were forcing people to leave their homes if there was the slightest accusation or worry that they were sick. In the middle of the night, small groups of men with sticks and bars were apparently going around 'to remove the infected', as their ringleader told me in an interview.

These people were seen as heroes in their local communities. They were nothing more than power hungry thugs who preyed on the weak, unfortunate and the poor.

The majority of the time, the groups would force the families out of their homes just so they could loot and rob the house of everything that was left behind. The family would leave everything bar necessities, like clothes and medications, and then the gangs would take all of their belongings and sell them.

These scumbags used the fear of the many to fleece the few.

The government's policy, as they spun it, was that the research was a way to help grow society and push it forward, but The Resistance and others saw it for what it really was – a way to keep the healthy population happy and productive.

The purging of the ill to areas away from the main population was simple – no one liked to see sick people, old people or people who were dependent on the rest of us. These people were no longer seen as a valuable resource that could be used by industry or businesses, so they were left on the periphery of society, looking in on the rest of us able bodied and healthy, wanting for a life that was out of reach.

They were spent – the forgotten.

I remember reading all of the stories of people who had been shifted and transported to the facilities out in the countryside. Some of them were nobodies, some were homeless, some were children, young adults, some were professionals with great intellects and some were even celebrities.

It didn't matter who you were, from the homeless man in the street to the multi-millionaire celebrity with everything anyone would ever want. Some of these new illnesses and diseases were seriously dangerous, and they were indiscriminate. Money and success cannot protect a human body from germs or viruses it comes into contact with. Neither can they protect from new genetic disorders and diseases that were built into the very body they degraded and limited more as each day went by.

We were all at risk and that was what scared everyone.

Seth explained that this was the reason for The Institute and the tests that went on there. The Authorities wanted to test the population for possible cures to emerging diseases and illnesses. This led to the Population Screening Initiative – PSI.

This was their best option, in their eyes, to screen everyone for the illnesses – removing them from the site immediately and away from the main population. They could also screen everyone for any possible genetic markers that showed an immunity to any of the emerging diseases on the World Health Organisation's radar.

The word was that the medical researchers had found a genome that was dormant within a small percentage of the population that could help cure certain illnesses and diseases that were spreading more rapidly throughout the world.

All of the nations linked up to research possible

cures for these threats, but this didn't stop the paranoia about how some countries were keeping some information from others. Russia claimed that America was allowing its people to suffer when they had a possible cure for an eye infection that led to rapid eye degeneration and even blindness that was spreading through St Petersburg. The Germans claimed that the French were withholding vital information researched about a flu-like virus that started to take hold in Stuttgart.

Some world leaders were sure other leaders were trying to let the illnesses spread like wildfire though their countries to weaken them enough to be taken over, but this was nonsense. In some extreme cases, this paranoia and hyping up of desperate people, led to unrest along borders. In Ukraine, the Russian army invaded and stormed a research facility in Kharkiv to capture a leading research scientist who had apparently had a breakthrough when researching an infectious skin condition that was being passed through touch and, when left untreated, could lead to patients needing skin grafts as skin would blister and need to be removed in the most extreme cases.

Of course, none of that nonsense was true. The researcher from Ukraine couldn't help the Russian people's skin condition and the flu-like virus was able to be treated by the German-led research.

The fact was that we were and are all made up of the same bones, muscles, blood and organs and the only way to beat these diseases was to ensure the country next to yours was healthy, not being ravaged by an epidemic.

The fact was that the world was at a crossing point. We could either work together to try and find a cure for what was threatening us, or we could tear each other apart while the new emerging diseases and illnesses wiped us out one by one. The beauty of the diseases was that they would get stronger while we as governments and nations fought over petty issues.

The problem The Resistance and others had with the whole process of screening the population was how they started to 'disappear' people and keep them prisoner to harvest whatever they could from them to help their research.

Some of the people were removed to the facilities away from the population but The Authorities could easily tell the families that's where they were, and it would be accepted. *The Authorities are keeping us safe*, is what they'd say. No one would question the fact that someone who was ill needed to be separated to keep everyone else safe.

Soon, stories emerged from families of sons, daughters, mothers, fathers, etcetera who were disappearing without a trace and no bodies being found.

Many of my sources at *The Tribune* shared stories like this time after time but I was never allowed to print the stories I got from the families as they were. I always had to change them.

'Incendiary' was the word my editor used to describe stories like this. Some people were afraid of fire, but I was always drawn to it, like a moth to the flame, I would be drawn towards danger and the truth – it intrigued me.

It was stories like this that drove me towards The Resistance and made me start to see things from their side – to believe their beliefs. When I started to doubt the world I was a part of, I soon became putty or clay in the hands of Seth, Carl and the others. They could mould me into whatever they wanted me to be.

I knew that at the time, I wasn't stupid or gullible, but I was tired of being told to look away from the truth when it was staring me right in the face. I wanted to turn and look, even just once, to see what was underneath the Iron Curtain that always seemed to be drawn around the incidents that involved the disappeared.

It is simply the right thing to do, the 'expert' exclaimed. *We are a population who face new risks each and every day. Burying our heads in the sand and hoping things will change is not enough. We have to be forward thinking and if that means making some difficult choices then so be it.*

The expert was a man called Dr George Mason, an expert in the field of disease control, who was always wheeled out by the health and research arms of The Authorities to make sure people saw their reasons why 'difficult choices had to be made' – this was his catchphrase. No choice ever seemed to be simple to make or even with a little consideration. The choices were always difficult.

Soon enough, my phone rang, and it was Carl. His picture shone up from the phone display just beside me, his face smiling at me while mine grimaced at the thought of having to pick up where we left off the night before.

"Hello," I said, instantly turning his call waiting picture into the live video call. If it were anyone else, I would have made myself more presentable but as it was Carl I let him see me as I was.

"Hi, were you sleeping?"

"No, I was just lying here listening to the news."

"Just the usual 'difficult choices' then?" he asked,

teasing a smile from me.

"As always."

We paused for a second, looking at each other, not knowing what to say next. Carl jumped straight to the reason he called to save the awkward pause, as always.

"Seth asked me to call you. It's time to put things in motion."

"I thought he would need more time to make plans."

"The plans were already there for another mission, so he wants to go soon. The way he sees it is the longer we leave it between your last visit to Iris and the one to free her, it will be more suspicious."

"No rest for the wicked then?"

Carl smiled. "You know better than that, Jade."

I smiled back. "I'll be in as soon as I can. Bye."

Carl's face faded to black and I rolled onto my back. *It's time to put things in motion*. Carl was really trying to morph into Seth. The more time Carl spent at The Resistance, the more his words were becoming Seth's words.

I knew I had to get up, it was inevitable. "Radio off," I called, hopping out of bed to get dressed.

CHAPTER 7

Everyone was in the room when I arrived. It was clear from the expressions on their faces that it was time. The range of emotions went from eager to anxious and from scared to determined. So many people around the table were scanning the eyes of those opposite them to see if they were feeling similar emotions to the person on the other side of the table.

The plans had all been laid previously for a separate extraction from The Institute six months beforehand so nothing much needed to be changed. The same people were to carry out the same roles and the same actions had to be carried out. I was the only change to the formula but, so long as I carried out my role as expected, everything should have gone according to plan.

I knew from the time I left Iris' recording with

Seth that he would want to carry out the mission as soon as possible. His eyes were easy to read. I respected him, but I couldn't help thinking that he was being somewhat reckless going in straight away for Iris and not giving us all time to consider the plans fully. Even though the plans were the same, there was one huge difference that could have changed everything – Iris.

The target they had in the previous mission was nowhere near as high profile or as important to The Authorities as Iris was. Iris was the chaos piece that could have made or broken the mission.

As I left my apartment, I packed a bag with some comfortable clothes, underwear and the uniform Seth gave me for The Institute. I knew that Seth could be impulsive, but I was confident that Carl and the other heads of The Resistance would not let him go ahead with any mission that was underprepared or could be dangerous for any of us or Iris for that matter.

If he decided to go then I was ready and, from the looks on the faces of everyone else, they were ready too. Carl looked pale, as though the blood had been drained from him, so I knew everything was prepared and that I was down to play an integral part in whatever it was.

Seth sat at the head of the rectangular table and Carl was sat on his left with Dr Rosen on his right. Annyagh, the hard-nosed tactician of The Resistance, was sat next to Dr Rosen.

I sat in the one seat that was left free at the end of the table opposite Seth and listened in to the conversation that was to continue.

"Thank you for joining us, Jade," Seth announced from the head of the table. "Let's continue."

The group discussed the intricate details of the plan. It was clear that everything had been thought about – what time it was to be carried out, who was in specific roles and who was in a supporting role in case something did go wrong, the weapons that were to be carried and who carried them, where Dr Rosen was to be just in case Iris needed him urgently and, of course, what I was to do, where I was to go and how I was to get Iris from her room to the ambulance.

The doubt I had when I initially sat down and looked at Seth was slowly dissipating. It still remained a little, simply because I was a sceptical person, but, after hearing the plan, I was confident that things had been prepared to the exact detail and, if anything happened, it was something we had no control over.

Dr Rosen was a large man. He was over six feet tall and a little overweight for his height. It was obvious that he had been retired as he had a gut that protruded over the waistband of his trousers. He had a short beard that was grey, like the remnants of the hair on his sides of his balding head. In his eyes, there was a warmth and it was obvious that he cared deeply for Iris.

I had never met him before but, from listening to him talk about Iris and his time at The Institute, it was clear that he deeply cared for her. To Dr Rosen, she was like a granddaughter.

While he spoke, his voice quivered with emotion at times – especially when he shared the stories about the more controversial, intrusive tests he was asked to carry out on such a young and sometimes frail body.

No one in the room spoke. Instead, we all sat and listened to the inner workings of The Institute and the effects Dr Rosen's work had on him mentally. "I was tortured. Most nights I didn't sleep. I remember pacing the floors the night before I had to carry out their instructions.

"Stefana would wake up and ask me what the matter was but I couldn't tell her at the start. I made up some story about feeling ill, having a headache or having to get up early to look over some papers before work.

"Deep down, I know she knew. It wasn't long before she cornered me about what was really going on. I don't remember much about the time before I finally opened up to her. I was sleep deprived and everything is a blur from then but, that morning, when I finally came clean with Stefana, everything is as clear as crystal.

"I was sat on the office chair in my study, staring at the wall in front of me. The door opened behind me and I mustn't have heard it, either that or I was resigned to the fact that Stefana knew something was bothering me and I had to be honest with her. She touched my shoulder and asked me to tell her what was wrong. With the tone of her voice, I knew there was no point in even trying to make up a story – thirty-five years of marriage will do that to a relationship."

A welcomed ripple of laughter rippled around the table and helped to lighten the story we were being told. Dr Rosen smiled and scanned round the table before he continued, making eye contact with each of us as he did, almost as a thank you for laughing at his light joke.

"I told Stefana everything. Even though I knew it

could put her in danger, I couldn't help it. I was broken.

"They broke me.

"Stefana didn't say anything, she didn't attempt to lie and tell me she understood because she couldn't. The fact was that the silence and listening ear she lent to me was enough. She sat opposite me, perched on the edge of my desk, holding my hand.

"I told her how ashamed I was. Ashamed of myself. Ashamed of what I did to Iris, but I also told Stefana how I was worried about her being ashamed of me – of what I'd become."

Dr Rosen stopped for a second and wiped a tear from his eye.

"She just looked at me and said she loved me. By looking into her eyes, I knew she meant that she would never have been ashamed of me doing my job. The fact that I was sitting there in the state I was in, Stefana knew my emotions were genuine.

"She also knew that I knew what had to be done. That day I went in and told the powers above me that I was to retire. I had never felt so relieved. A weight had been lifted from my shoulders and, that evening, I left work smiling for the first time in a long time.

"I drove home to tell Stefana the news and found her in the kitchen, lying face down on the floor. She was gone.

"At first I suspected that someone from The Authorities had been listening in – it wasn't uncommon that they would have surveillance outside disgruntled figures' houses – but that wasn't the case.

"Stefana had a massive heart attack no more than an hour after I had left for work that morning."

Dr Rosen had started to sob to himself. He took a few seconds to compose himself before finishing off what he had come to say that day. There was no doubt that his words had impacted us.

We all believed every word that came out of his mouth. The power of his emotion and the genuine tone of his voice was enough to sway even the most doubting of Resistance members about what we were about to do.

"The guilt I felt that day, and every day since then has hung like a weight around my neck. They took everything from me. My career. My love. My life." Dr Rosen looked around the table. "Now it's time I take something back."

The room sat silent for a moment as his words hung in the air, like clouds, dissipating to fill the space between us, breathing it in, and becoming part of us.

Seth stood up and was the first and only one of us to shatter the silence. "I think we all know what needs to be done. The time is now."

The room emptied swiftly, and I followed Annyagh, no doubt the person to see to get information about what was to happen at the sharp end of the operation at The Institute – the sharp end that I knew directly involved me.

"I didn't miss much, did I?"

"No, nothing important. Just the fact that we have heard, from one of our sources inside The Institute, that they're planning to move Iris tomorrow."

"Wait, tomorrow? Do they…?"

"No, they aren't onto you, okay?" Annyagh led me by the arm into the toilets and locked the door behind us. "Listen, I know you're probably strung out since you were at The Institute last, but you did a good job." I couldn't hide the surprised expression on my face from this woman who never had a kind word to say about anyone, especially me. "Our source told us that they are planning a series of new tests on Iris in the coming weeks and they are going to move her to another facility in the Shetland Islands to carry out the research.

"This means that they have to move her, keep her sedated, move everything that she needs and ensure she settles before the new tests can begin.

"Word is that they want to give her a week or so to settle to make sure there are no 'complications' – whatever that means."

"What are the tests?" I asked.

"We don't know. Dr Rosen thinks they are a series of more intrusive tests, intracranial tests. Apparently, they were lined up before he left, and they could have implications."

"Like what?"

"I don't understand all the science behind it, but it involves extracting brain matter and the worry is that Iris could be 'damaged' as a result."

"So we need to act?"

"We need to act. Let's go get ready." Annyagh unlocked the door and left in her usual, butch, purposeful stride.

This was a side to her that I knew all too well when I first came to The Resistance. She was very rude, barely spoke to me and, when she did, she usually had some horrible, derogatory comment to make. When it was obvious that I was committed to the cause,

Annyagh started to soften towards me and would even talk to me about my relationship with Carl.

Once I'd proven myself, Annyagh showed me her true self.

I followed Annyagh out of the room, and the butterflies inevitably and uncontrollably started to flutter. Immediately, my mind started to wander. What if they caught me? What if I forgot something? What if Iris refused to come with me and she started calling for help? I knew I had the type of personality that would overanalyse everything, but I also had to force myself to remember that Annyagh, Seth, Carl and Dr Rosen wouldn't have left anything to chance.

I had to trust them, and I did.

CHAPTER 8

The moon was beautiful in the sky. It hung like a perfectly spherical lantern glowing warmly in the night sky, lighting up the dark streets with a pale blue/white hue. I don't know what it was about moonlight like that during late night walks – it always calmed me.

Ever since I was a little girl, I loved taking myself out in the dead of night and sitting in the pitch-black darkness of our back garden. I knew I was too little to go walking in the streets at that time of night, but the moonlight was like a friend who was always there when you needed them.

I would sit for what felt like hours in my pyjamas looking up at the moon and the stars that enveloped the cratered orb, ensuring it had company in the infinite darkness but not intruding so much as to steal its spotlight.

I loved those nights as a little girl. The calm that fell over me was as silent and painless as the creeping cold that would work its way up my body from my feet, up my shins to my knees and eventually my whole body, forcing me to go back into bed where I would cocoon myself, like a caterpillar, waiting for sleep to take me.

The tiny gap in the curtain would allow me to keep an eye on my soothing moon as my skin prickled back to something resembling life from the cold that had deadened it outside. The pacifying moon would soon nurse me to sleep and I would sleep soundly knowing that she was there watching over me.

My guardian from on high.

The usual hum of cars was the only movement around me. The night was eerily still and there was not even a breeze to stir the leaves on the trees. It felt as though some higher power was either freezing time to allow my journey to be uninterrupted or holding his breath ahead of the chaos that was about to ensue.

In the end, I found out which one of those it was but, at that moment in time, I would never have known how successful my mission would be.

The Institute's lights lit up the sky, like a beacon

rising up from the city around – a shining light to the world proclaiming, 'We are here to save you.'

The other buildings in the area were dulled down in the evening as The Authorities tried to save energy but the beacon of The Institute was always lit up no matter what. Everyone was convinced that The Authorities lit it to give us all hope that what the doctors and researchers were doing there was worthy and just.

They were our lighthouse, lighting the way through the darkness.

The closer I got to the building, the more butterflies started to hatch from their cocoons and flutter around inside my abdomen. I worked hard on controlling my breathing to stay calm, but it was hard when I knew the weight of the mission I was undertaking. This mission was the one we knew could crack open The Authorities and The Institute for good and people all over the country and the world would see them for what they were – evil, immoral snakes.

The security guard on the gate was new. He was a man in his fifties with a hardened expression, as though he had seen a lot of things that I, and not many other people, had seen. No doubt he was tired and probably disinterested in me and every other person who passed through the gate that night.

As I walked in through the gate and scanned my ID on the sensor, the gate opened slowly, and the security guard simply nodded at my entry.

It was as though this gesture was a blessing as I passed by. The gatekeeper allowed my safe passage.

I smiled and nodded as I passed, then I swiftly made my way to the main entrance and the elevator. The same elevator I used the night I first met Iris. In my mind, I kept seeing the doctor and nurse coming down the corridor as they waited for the elevator to come. A part of me could not help but visualise the pair of them waiting for me when the doors of the elevator opened once I had reached Iris' floor.

The closer I got to Iris' room, I became more nervous and my mind started to picture things and catastrophise over every step of the mission that I knew was to come.

Soon enough, the elevator doors opened and to my relief the corridor outside was deserted. No doctor. No nurse. Just a series of locked doors that led to many faceless beings undoubtedly being tested and experimented on by The Institute. I knew that so many of these innocent people deserved our help just as much as Iris did, but I was not here for them – I was there for Iris.

I stepped out of the elevator and looked up to the corner of the corridor opposite me, the LED light on the security camera blinked on and off with a pale blue colour – this was the pre-programmed signal from Carl that he had hacked into the security system. The blue light was a sign that he had embedded the pre-recorded loop so that the security guards of The Institute would not know that I had even been there.

I walked to Iris' door and scanned my key card. A dull click let me know that the door was opened so I stepped swiftly inside and closed it behind me. Iris lay on the bed – she was sleeping.

Outside Iris' door, I could hear the faint noise of service alarms from the beds of patients at the far end of the adjoining corridor calling any nurse on the floor to help. The alarms were like the call of birds in a forest, all chirping in a similar tone but at differing times, ensuring they all had their own airtime to sing to the world.

This was my sign, my cue to get Iris and make my way down to the waiting ambulance. I knew that Annyagh and Seth were in the ambulance waiting for me. The Resistance's contact had arranged it so that the escape ambulance was not detected as being a suspicious vehicle. Like me, Seth and Annyagh had been given passes, uniforms, and the ambulance had been fitted with an official sensor and serial number that would open and close gates as well as grant the drivers access to the restricted compounds inside The Institute.

The contact had really thought of everything. They had given us everything apart from Iris herself. That was up to us to achieve. The doors were literally opened for us to walk through, now we just had to take the steps while dodging any traps and prying eyes that may befall us.

As I approached Iris' bedside, I was unable to take my eyes off her. She lay there motionless. I could barely even see the rise and fall of her chest as she breathed. Her arms were strapped down to the bed by belts at her wrists and her legs were strapped down by belts at her ankles.

The more I looked at Iris, I started to wonder. The contact had said that Iris had to be drugged and sedated ahead of her move to the Shetlands research site, so why was it necessary to strap her down?

For a long time, I was not able to fully recall what happened in the room with Iris that evening. It was as though my body was on autopilot, being controlled by some inner being, like a puppet-master was tugging on my strings to move every sinew, joint, limb and even thought that flickered and sparked through my body.

As I look back, I knew that I had just rehearsed the whole mission in my head so many times that my body knew it better than my mind did. I was always a thorough person right the way from childhood until my working life as a journalist. I had to make sure things were done meticulously because, if I didn't, I would always question how I went about it if I failed.

I didn't like failure, and, in the case of Iris, failure wasn't an option.

The room was completely silent and in almost total darkness, like it was all in some alternative reality. My breathing was very loud and every time I inhaled or exhaled, the noise was almost deafening. I expected that every time I exhaled I would wake Iris up and she would panic, then hit the service button to call any genuine nurse and doctor to her room within seconds.

My weight distorted the shape of the mattress on the bed and I started talking to her. I can't remember exactly what I said but I remember I was trying to make sure she knew I was there to help her, to free her from whatever existence it was that she had found herself in.

As I spoke to her, whispering gently into her ear, I undid the straps on her wrists and ankles to free her. That night, when I said I was there to get her out and I promised her that I would protect her, I swore I saw a slight smile rise and fall on the corner of her mouth, like the sudden break of a wave on a calm, motionless beach.

I lifted and placed Iris into the wheelchair in the corner of her room. I strapped her in and wrapped her in a blanket to keep her warm. The tablet computer on the end of her bed was flashing. I picked it up and saw a window with a streaming status bar and I knew that Carl was uploading the next stage of the extraction.

Dr Rosen made it clear that before Iris could go to the separate Shetlands facility, she would have to go through some tests to check that she was well enough to make the trip.

The file that Carl was uploading to Iris' tablet was the document that gave details of the checks that the doctors would do to her – some invasive, some not. Either way, I had the documents to get Iris from her room and down to the ground floor.

The plan was to get Iris to the south corridor and then out of a fire door. From there, we would get her into the ambulance where Seth and Annyagh were waiting.

My heart was pounding, making the entire cavity of my chest thud and reverberate with the muscle's beats. I could hear the beats in my head and, if I listened carefully enough, I could swear I heard the rushing of blood in my arteries and veins as it flooded through my body at pressure.

I opened the door quietly and slowly.

Outside the door, it sounded clear. The only noise was that of voices calling and feet shuffling down at the far end of the corridor. I felt somewhat at ease that the doctors and nurses were still preoccupied with Carl's diversion, trying to attend to service alarms going off in rooms of patients at the furthest points away from Iris' room.

Lights in the corridor were still lit and the blue light of the security camera was still flashing. It was up to me now to make the move to get Iris out of the room and into the elevator.

I took a deep breath, opened my eyes and strolled out of the room, pushing Iris into the elevator with the confidence of a nurse who had done this for years. I felt that the more confident I appeared on the outside, the less likely I would be stopped for looking suspicious or that I looked as though I shouldn't be there.

I needed to look like I belonged.

The door of the elevator closed, and we descended. Iris still had not moved since I sat her into the wheelchair. She sat motionless, comatose with no expression on her face as her head hung limp, chin on her chest.

I started to feel anger rise in me for the fact that this young girl was so drugged that she was unable to move or register any kind of signs of life other than breathing. This was no way for a young life to be treated.

The door opened on the ground floor, and I walked out towards the south corridor, opposite the doors of the elevator.

I remembered, from the plans of the building, that I had to make my way down the south corridor to a fire door that was just before the end, on the right-hand side. This door led to the car park where Seth and Annyagh were waiting for us.

The main entrance way was near deserted apart from a nurse sitting typing on her screen. She was in her fifties and struggled to see what was on the screen never mind details about me, what I looked like or who it was I was pushing in the wheelchair.

The nurse was portly, with a face that looked barely wrinkled, like she had been pumped up so much that the wrinkles were stretched out from the inside, like a wrinkled balloon. She had a kind face. The kind of face that would reassure you as a patient under her care. Her light blue uniform was pristinely pressed and bore a nametag and her nurse's watch.

The tablet from Iris' room was loaded with a file that Dr Rosen and Carl put together that stated I was to take Iris to a test room at the bottom of the south corridor in preparation for her trip to the next facility. Everything that was on the tablet was taken from the official documents that Dr Rosen still had and fed to The Resistance for use in such missions as this. I knew that if I was stopped by a nurse or doctor that I was to show them the tablet and they would believe that everything was above board and official.

The whole of The Institute was still buzzing, trying to tend to many of the service alarms that were still ringing around the wards. I nodded and smiled to the nurse in the office in the main entrance. She smiled and waved at me, probably glad to see another human face instead of the font and images of the documents she was viewing on the screens in front of her.

The south corridor was quiet. I looked up at the cameras in the corner of the corridor and noted that the light blue light was still flashing – Carl was there, watching over me.

The fire door was no more than ten metres to my right. My heart started to pound harder the nearer I got to the door. My feet felt heavy and time almost started to slow down.

My feet shuffled automatically towards the emergency exit when my attention was drawn to a door opening to my left. A doctor made his way out of the room and walked towards me, carrying a folder while adjusting his neck tie.

As he approached me, his eyes met mine and we both smiled at each other. He was not much taller than me, was tan skinned and had a face of dark black stubble that he wore like a badge of honour to show that he had been on a long shift.

"Is this young lady ready for her tests ahead of the big move?" the doctor asked.

"Yes, she's such an easy patient to look after," I replied.

"She will be great. She always is." The doctor stopped and started talking to me. "What tests do we have lined up for her this time?"

He lifted up the tablet computer started scanning the uploaded documents from Carl.

"They're just trying to be thorough."

"We always are, us doctors." He continued to scan the tablet screen. "They really are putting you through the mill this time, aren't they Iris?"

The doctor put the tablet back and squeezed Iris' upper arm caringly with his hand. It came across to me that he really cared about her. "Do you treat Iris often?"

"No, I used to. Now I work with only adult subjects."

Intrigued by this, I paused for a second. "How come?"

The young doctor looked around him and swallowed. "Let's just say that working with Iris was wonderful, but I couldn't hurt her anymore."

"I see what you mean."

"You had better get her to the treatment room, they'll be expecting you and they *hate* waiting," the young doctor replied. "I'm sorry for keeping you."

"Oh, don't worry. I think I'm early anyway."

I stood at the door to the treatment room and thumbed my key card until the doctor exited the door and made his way towards the lift.

As soon as he was out of sight, I turned and walked briskly to the emergency exit.

I rested my hand on the bar of the door and closed my eyes as I pushed it, half expecting a deafening fire alarm to go off, alerting every doctor, nurse and security guard in The Institute to the door and my whereabouts. I pushed the bar and the latch clicked open.

No alarm.

I breathed a sigh of relief and wheeled Iris out onto the wheelchair ramp, closing the door gently behind me. I looked around me for the ambulance driven by Seth and Annyagh and, sure enough, it was right where it was supposed to be. Seth got out. The ramp lowered, and the back door of the ambulance opened, almost greeting us with open arms.

I wheeled Iris into the ambulance. The ramp raised, and the doors sealed us inside.

Iris was still motionless, sleeping – like a doll. She was beautiful. I looked at her face, peaceful and still as it was, and wondered what was going on inside her head. What was she dreaming? Did she dream? Was the real Iris lost forever, even if Dr Rosen counteracted the treatments he and others had carried out at The Institute?

There were so many unanswered questions that I wanted to answer and answer as soon as possible.

The front door of the ambulance closed with a thud and the engine fired up. Annyagh drove off, sirens and lights off, out the gate and past the security guard, removing Iris from the only life she'd known and leading us to what we hoped was safety.

CHAPTER 9

She was sitting on the edge of the bed, almost motionless. She looked odd in the clothes we'd given her. The jeans and T-shirt made her look like a typical teenager, insecure in herself and what was happening to her.

As I watched her, I couldn't help but wonder how much of a struggle it was for her being away from The Institute. It was all that she knew – her life. The four walls of that room and the select few rooms she was taken to for tests were all that she had experienced and all that she remembered.

Iris was unable to take her eyes off what was happening outside. I looked out to see what it was that she watched but it was nothing in particular.

Life was happening.

People walked. Children played. Cars drove and

stopped and drove again when the traffic lights allowed it. Birds flew from building to building, some playing games as they glided through the streets.

Iris' eyes simply took it all in.

"So this is outside," she asked in her monotonic tone with almost no body to the words that were being propelled from her mouth.

"Yes."

She paused for a time, simply breathing and scanning all that she saw. "Things just… happen?"

"Yes, I suppose so," I replied, not wanting to fill her head with confusion about The Authorities, the world the government had built, etcetera. I just wanted to keep Iris' understanding of what she saw to what it was — new and innocent.

She turned to look at me. "What is your name?"

"Jade."

"Like the colour."

"Like the colour," I replied, smiling and trying to make Iris feel secure.

"You were at the hospital before."

"Yes, I was," I replied. This confirmation that she remembered me was comforting but I was unsure to what extent she remembered her encounter with me in her room in The Institute. Did she remember me clearly, as in remember every single word she said and every word that I said in return? On the other hand, did she barely remember anything about me? Was I nothing more than a mirage in the desert to Iris, shimmering and luring her in just in time to disappear into thin air?

I watched Iris as she paused, contemplating the fact that she had just learned. "Were you there for me?"

I paused for a short beat, just considering my answer for a second before uttering it. "I was."

Iris turned her head slowly and looked at me, studying me. "Why did you come to get me?"

Unsure how to answer, I told her a semi-truth. "There are some people who are desperate to meet you."

"Meet me? Why me?"

Considering my answer carefully again, I paused slightly. "You are important to them."

With my reply, a light appeared to blink and flicker slightly within Iris' head, as though a distant memory was awakening. "Doctors?"

"Yes."

"I have known many doctors. Some of them grew old and said they were leaving but would see me again soon. I miss them. They were very kind to me as I grew up." Iris paused for a short time, returning to look out the window, almost looking out for the visitors that were promised to her. "Are they on their way?"

"They will be here soon."

"How soon?"

"Not for a while so I think it is best you get some rest."

Iris nodded and lay down on the bed, closing her eyes instantly. Almost as soon as she closed her eyes, her breathing deepened and she was asleep within minutes.

The life she lived was one of total control and she was used to being told what to do and, from what Seth and the others at The Resistance knew, the medication she was given was used to suppress many of the normal qualities and characteristics people outside in the 'real world' had and expressed.

I messaged Seth and the others to let them know how Iris was doing and that she was resting. I knew that with texting Seth and not messaging Carl, I could be facing another argument when I next saw him, but I'd had enough of his jealousy and he had to accept that I had a role now within The Resistance whether he liked it or not.

Between messages hours passed but I was too anxious and filled with adrenaline to sleep. My attention was split between the messages to Seth, the world outside and Iris, sleeping on the bed opposite me.

Occasionally, she would let out moans and talk in her sleep. The words were spoken so softly I was unable to make out what she was saying, but I listened intently, just in case I could understand even the slightest fragment of her unconscious conversations.

These utterings, these windows into Iris' subconscious were intriguing to me. As far as details went, The Resistance knew very little about what exactly went on inside The Institute with Iris and the other subjects who were tested on. I sat on the edge of my bed, staring intently at Iris' lips, hoping to glean the slightest detail from the tongues that she was speaking in her dreams.

As I watched her, I could only make out slight fragments – *I'm cold, Mummy, stop, I want to go outside,* etcetera. In the time I sat listening to her, there was nothing of use that I could share with Seth and The Resistance. I also came to the realisation that inside Iris' head was a complex entangled web of thoughts, memories and emotions and the world outside The Institute was a daunting one.

She needed me and I would be there for her for as long as she needed me.

The next morning, I woke up to find Iris awake and staring at me from her bed. "Where are we, Jade?" she asked in a matter-of-fact tone.

"You're safe, Iris," I replied, sitting up, unsure what to expect next. There was a different look about Iris. Her eyes were the same silver, but they moved with more purpose and she held her knees tight up into her chest, like a little child, terrified and in need of assurance. "It's just you and I for the minute. Don't worry. I'm not going to hurt you."

"Why am I here? Where are the nurses? Where are the doctors?" She was becoming more upset as the reality started to hit her. Tears started to form in her startled eyes. The pink and red that started to tint the white of her eye only made the silver irises stand out more.

I got out of my bed and sat next to her. "They

aren't here, Iris. I'm here to look after you, don't worry."

"Why am I here?"

"I can't answer all of your questions, but I promise it'll all be okay. We are here together, just us, and nothing is going to happen to you." Iris looked at me, her eyes filled with confusion and uncertainty. I put my arm around her and she leant into me.

Iris trusted me. When she looked at me, she saw someone who cared about her, who knew how scared she was and would do anything for her. As I held her into me, she shivered, and her hand gripped onto my side.

"What's happening to me, Jade?" Iris asked.

I answered, pausing to consider how to word what was actually happening to her. I couldn't tell her that she was a pawn in a game between The Resistance and The Authorities. I couldn't tell her that we'd saved her from a life of captivity and experimentation. I had to tell her the simplest form of the truth that I could muster. "You're free."

"I don't feel right," Iris replied, placing the palm of her opened hand against her forehead and rubbing it, attempting to soothe herself.

I paused before replying. I didn't want to immediately tell her it may have been withdrawal from the medications she was having pumped into her. I just wanted to let her talk. As far as I was concerned, I was there to listen and answer what I felt I could and wouldn't scare her. "How do you mean?"

"I don't know," she continued. "Behind my eyes feels hot and fuzzy and my fingers are tingling." She rubbed her hands together slowly, as though she were trying to rub away the pins and needles.

"You're just over-tired. Don't worry. Those feelings will pass as you get more rest."

Iris looked up at me and smiled slightly to show she understood. I couldn't tell her about the medication. She was dealing with enough change without me adding to it.

When Seth and The Resistance looked into the medication, the doctor who looked after Iris originally, Dr Rosen, assured us that the withdrawal would pass within a few weeks. He would also bring some other drugs to relieve the symptoms Iris would be experiencing.

As far as Dr Rosen was concerned, he was just helping Iris cope with the transition into her new life, even if that meant drugging her himself. He had sworn that he wouldn't be a part of the mess that he had helped create at The Institute, but he had a moral duty to help Iris return to a normal existence. Two wrongs don't make a right but, in this case, Dr Rosen's 'wrong' was slightly closer to the centre line between okay and wrong. The game Dr Rosen was about to re-enter was a complex one and he had to guide Iris back from the wilderness she had become stranded in.

Iris sat at the kitchen table and I put a bowl of cereal in front of her as I sat opposite her with my own bowl. She picked up the spoon and ate readily.

Iris was like a typical fifteen-year-old girl but with silver in her eyes instead of blue, brown or green. The more I saw of Iris, the more I saw myself in her. She was a girl who was unsure of herself but had a real fire within her that was only just beginning to spark into life.

"What is it?" she asked with a mouthful of cereal.

I smiled. "It's good to see you eating."

"I'm so hungry," she replied, struggling to keep the half-chewed food in her mouth.

"If you need more just ask and I can make you something else." I started to eat, using the time as I chewed to prepare myself for what may happen after

I said my next sentence. "Later today, we're going to try something new."

"New? Like what?"

"Well, I thought we could try dying and cutting our hair a little."

"How little is 'a little'?"

"Enough to make us look a little different." I had another spoonful of cereal. "We'll wait until we see the colour. You can choose if you like." I didn't really care what colour Iris chose, so long as we got rid of the light blonde hair that made her stand out more than Seth and The Resistance needed when it came to the next step – hiding her until the time was right to expose the truth about the whole gene programme. I knew that Dr Rosen's face and presence in the room would help Iris see that we were trying to help her. It would confirm to her that we were looking after her.

"Dark brown?"

"I think we can do that."

"Can we both have the same?"

I smiled and looked at the warmth in Iris' face as she awaited my reply. "Sure, why not?"

After breakfast, we went to the bathroom and dyed our hair. As I massaged the dye into Iris' hair, I started humming a song my mother used to sing to me.

"What's that?" Iris asked.

"It's a song my mum used to sing to me when I was a little girl."

"Sing it aloud."

Immediately, I felt my face begin to glow red with embarrassment at the thought of singing aloud for someone I hardly knew. "Oh, I don't know…"

"Please, it sounds lovely."

I sang the song as I finished Iris' hair. She never took her eyes off me in the reflection of the mirror. Every so often, Iris smiled as I repeated the chorus of the song over again.

At times like that, it hit me that she had such little experience of normality. Things as simple as singing were alien to her. Whether she had done them before was irrelevant as she had been controlled with so much medication over the years. All I knew was that I took it upon myself, from then on, to do what I could to let her have as many normal experiences as our situation would allow us.

I finished up my own hair and Iris sat at the kitchen table playing card games until the dye set and changed our appearance sufficiently before washing it out. The simple games like Blackjack, Jack Change It and Snap were very basic, but they made Iris smile and laugh like I had never seen before.

We rinsed our hair out in the bathroom and cut our long hair styles into chin-length bobs. Iris looked very different, but she was still beautiful. Her eyes would have to be hidden with contact lenses when Seth and the other members of The Resistance came, but they shone as a reminder of the steely character she had inside.

Soon enough, the knock came on the door – two quick knocks, two knocks with longer gaps between and finally two further quick knocks. The feeling in my stomach was one of nausea. What if they caught Seth and he told them the knock code? What if they had found us? What would they do to me?

I chained the door and peeked out to see who it was. I opened the door the slightest crack to peek out – there was Annyagh, dressed typically in her butch, all-black appearance – "It's okay, babe, you can let us in."

I opened the door and Annyagh stepped in, slowly to ensure her normal, confident, strong style wouldn't scare Iris, making her think that she was going to be taken again. Annyagh totally softened her whole demeanour and walked over to Iris, kneeling down in front of her. "Hey, pretty girl, I love the hair." Annyagh ran her finger tips through Iris' dark brown hair. "I wish I had hair long enough to make it worth dyeing like yours."

Iris smiled nervously in acknowledgement, sat still, pinned to the bed with nerves at the experience of seeing these new faces stream in through the door. Her eyes danced from each new face and back to me, almost to seek my approval as to whether these people were trustworthy or not. *It's okay*, I mouthed to her.

Iris nodded but I could still sense an air of trepidation about her. After all, everyone in her life, up until now, were doctors and nurses – people whom she knew were paid to look after her. I knew she seemed to trust me but these other people being introduced to her was something she had never experienced before. Add to that the fact that she was experiencing all of this while coming off a cocktail of drugs for the first time meant that she was highly alert and suspicious of her surroundings.

I looked out through the opened door and the next face to see Iris was a familiar one, Dr Rosen. His eyes were pink with emotion that he was holding back, like a torrent of water behind a dam. I knew by looking at him that he deeply cared about this girl. He saw her as his own child in many ways and I know, deep inside, he felt guilty and beat himself up about the awful treatments he had to carry out in the name of The Institute and The Authorities.

I smiled at him and nodded, motioning for him to enter the room. I was doing all I could to reassure him that she was here and she was safe.

Dr Rosen walked in, almost tip-toeing into the room over egg shells, unsure of what reaction, if any at all, he would receive from this young girl.

When Iris saw him, she froze.

Dr Rosen stood in the doorway, medical bag in hand, and looked into those brilliant silver eyes that pierced him from across the room.

The silence in the room was palpable – like a giant heartbeat, it pounded and grew louder with each millisecond that passed. The air thickened and none of us wanted to breathe it in, unsure of what would happen next.

"It's me, Iris," Dr Rosen whispered, his voice wobbling under the strain of emotion.

Iris didn't speak.

Iris didn't take her eyes off Dr Rosen, not even to me to look for reassurance.

Iris knew him.

Iris remembered.

"You remember me, don't you?"

Iris remained frozen.

"You were a little girl when we first met."

Nothing.

"You were so scared. You took my hand and held it so tightly. Your hands were freezing cold. Don't you remember?"

Iris' eyes started to redden – a light pink hue bled into the porcelain white of her eye.

Dr Rosen's emotions started to get the better of him. He knew there was a part of her that knew him. "We would play chess. You always wanted to be white, it was lucky you said. The games would last for weeks, wouldn't they? You would study the board endlessly between the times we played and plan every move in advance."

Iris' eyes shed a single tear, which she caught with a swift swipe of a hand.

Dr Rosen did the same, his voice shaking now he added, "I never stood a chance against you. You would beat me every time, but I wouldn't care. To see you grow, to see you develop was my reward."

"Where did you go?" Iris asked in a voice that was slightly louder than a whisper but tinted with the slightest amount of venom, so Dr Rosen knew she remembered who he was and the promise he broke.

Dr Rosen stood silently, paralysed by the words he knew he was bound to hear if Iris remembered him.

"You left me," Iris paused, wiping tears away from her eyes, trying to hold back the impossible. "Every day, I waited for you to come back but you didn't. Where did you go?"

"They made me leave you, Iris." Dr Rosen did his best to hold himself together as he explained himself to the girl before him. "They wanted me to do things to you, things I didn't agree with. I didn't want to hurt you. The tests would cause you pain and…"

"I thought…"

"I know what you probably thought. I know you felt abandoned and alone at the fact that I wasn't there to look after you, but they would have…"

The pair stopped and looked at each other, tears

streaming and a world between them that needed to be repaired but not in front of strangers like us.

In the corner, Annyagh did all she could to hold back any emotion, not allowing it to surface, but I could see that she was struggling. Seth and Carl couldn't look. Seth never cried but Carl was as soft as cotton wool. He was biting his lip, struggling to keep it together.

Iris stood up and stepped towards Dr Rosen who strode towards her, knelt down and held her into his chest. Iris wrapped her arms around Dr Rosen's neck and the pair of them stood in an embrace weeping.

Annyagh, Carl and Seth left, giving Dr Rosen, Iris and I some time. Carl, gathering himself together, gestured with his hand to call him and I nodded.

The door clicked closed and I was left in the room with Dr Rosen and Iris. The only sounds were mumbling and sniffling. I knew Iris felt safer with this man. He was all she knew for most of her life and, now that he was back, I knew she would fully trust me.

She would know I would never harm her.

CHAPTER 10

I was unable to sleep. I lay on the bed and fretted over every noise and bump I heard from outside or from the other apartments in the building. I knew all of the people in the building were sympathisers to The Resistance's cause, but it still didn't make me feel any less anxious. In my mind we were the most wanted people in the country and the Security Forces would scour the city and then the country to find Iris and I.

This made me consider our appearances even more.

I spent the next day spraying us with fake tan and playing card games with Iris to pass the time. Occasionally, we would just sit and look out the window at the world racing by.

Iris was extremely inquisitive. She wanted to know

what many of the strange things she saw happening were and why they may have been happening.

At times, I got frustrated but had to remember that she had spent much of her life in a secure facility and had little or no experience of the outside world.

It was pretty much all new to her.

At about three in the afternoon, Iris went quiet on the bed beside me when I was reading to her. Her whole body went limp and her breathing was deep and rhythmic. I was glad she fell asleep. She had been through so much those two days that the best thing I thought she could do was rest.

I had never been a big sister, but I felt that was the relationship I had to have with Iris. She had no one but I was determined to be that someone – the person she could rely on no matter what.

I felt that Seth and The Resistance needed her for their plans of exposing The Authorities for what they were, but I didn't want them to exploit her. It doesn't matter how just someone's intentions are, anyone is capable of exploiting anyone else for their own ends. Seth and The Resistance were no different, they were equally as susceptible to becoming corrupt as any other group of people who were united for the same cause. If I didn't protect her, would she be any better off with us than she was in The Institute?

Power was like money – it could corrupt even the kindest heart.

I almost felt as though I was caught in the middle, between a rock and a hard place. Through my short time in The Resistance, my eyes were opened up to the wrongs of the modern world and what The Authorities were willing to do to secure their own goals and plans, but I was a journalist and I always knew that no organisation, whether it be The Resistance or The Authorities, was whiter than white. Every organisation had the capacity to do wrong to achieve a right in the corrupt, modern dystopia we lived in.

I looked up to Seth, but I knew there was something he wasn't telling me. I always had a sixth sense for people keeping things from me. There was something about their eyes and how they looked at me when we spoke. Their eyes seemed to be looking around the room, anywhere but into mine, as though they were looking for someone else to save them from the conversation they didn't want to be having.

Iris was asleep when Seth and the others came later that day. I got a text to say they would be arriving shortly and I watched out the window for them approaching.

Outside, it was a hive of activity. The worker bees all buzzed around, carrying out their own jobs and roles in the hive. No one looked out of place. Each and every person buzzing round wore their own version of a black and yellow uniform – a conforming attire that showed all of the other worker bees, but more importantly the Queen Bee, that they were fitting into the plan set out for them.

When Seth appeared from around a corner across the street with Carl and Annyagh, they too did their best to fit into the swarms outside. It was clear that they didn't want to attract attention to themselves, but also to myself and Iris when they entered the building.

Each of them was dressed in dark grey boiler suits that were 'donated' by a sympathiser who owned a prominent electricity repair business. When Seth, Carl and Annyagh were on a mission, they regularly used uniforms of utility companies as they were as effective as camouflage. Everyone needed internet, electricity, television, etcetera so it only made sense to play the part of someone who fixed everything everyone was dependent on.

It was like having a skeleton key to every building in the country.

Carl and Annyagh were experts in the tech side of The Resistance and were behind much of the planning and execution of the mission to get me inside The Institute and out without detection – so far at least.

Annyagh was carrying a black backpack, Carl a large tool kit, each 'donated' by the utility repair company, and Seth carried nothing, as usual.

So many people looked at Seth as some kind of 'Jesus Christ figure' – a messiah, who was there to deliver some promised land, but Seth was just a man and I could see through him to some of his less than positive traits. I think Seth knew this and this was why he was normally up front with me, but, with Iris, he still hadn't opened up to share what his fascination was with her.

When I opened the door, Seth didn't say a word, he simply peered past me to look at Iris' sleeping body on the bed. He made his way over and knelt beside the bed, stroking her head. Iris didn't move. The only motion there was, was the rising and falling of her chest as she breathed.

Annyagh made her way in purposefully, winking at me as she passed, and Carl stood silently, awaiting my instruction to enter. We still weren't on the best of terms since we had that argument, but he knew he needed to carry on with his role and give one hundred percent or else Seth would find someone else to do it for him.

Carl was too proud to apologise, but he was also too proud of his own ability to let someone else swan in and take over the propaganda side of The Resistance.

If there was one thing I loved about Carl, it was his loyalty to something or someone he cared about. I knew he still loved me and I knew he wouldn't see anyone else until I made it absolutely clear we were finished. The truth was I wasn't sure I wanted us to finish. I just had too much to contend with at that time with the mission, Iris and Carl's paranoia – Carl's paranoia was the only thing I could let go.

As Iris slept, we discussed the rest of the plan. We would need some time to allow things to die down ahead of revealing the government's true intentions with their Population Screening Initiative.

I also needed some time to arrange a more permanent solution to myself and Iris' situation. I knew when I took up the mission at The Institute that my life was over in Hexingham, whether I liked it or not.

I knew I would have to leave Jade behind – she was dead now.

Annyagh took out a pair of smart glasses and programmed them to slightly change my eye shape as well as their colour from an onlooker's perspective. It was odd seeing me with different hair, darker skin and brown eyes. For me, the change was extreme, but I knew, for Iris, the change would be the polar opposite of what she had seen every day. She would look totally different – something that was essential for what we had planned.

I woke Iris and briefly explained what was happening. She accepted what was happening incredibly well, better than I expected, but she also seemed to be excited by what was unfolding in front of her. She looked at Seth and the others as friends as soon as she saw them with Dr Rosen. The connection between both groups allowed Iris to show an immediate trust in Seth, Annyagh and Carl.

Annyagh opened up her backpack and took out some clothes for myself and Iris, as well as some accessories to make her look like a normal fifteen-year-old girl.

When she came out of the bathroom changed into the clothes and wearing the glasses Annyagh had brought for her, she was unrecognisable. Her long near-white hair, silver eyes and pale skin had been changed to shoulder-length dark hair, tanned skin and deep brown eyes.

The plan was to make us look like sisters and the team at The Resistance had done an amazing job. The plans that we had discussed around the table that evening in Bethlehem were all meticulously planned out, and they were coming to fruition.

As Iris and I stood in front of the wardrobe mirror, a full-length sliding door, I put my arm around her to make her feel more comfortable with the whole experience, but it also made me realise just how alike we were.

Soon, the team left, and Iris and I were left alone with our new identities – I was Charlotte Payne and Iris was Erica Payne. The whole night, we spent our time talking and, as we did, we used our pseudonyms. From the moment Seth and the others left, we were no longer Jade and Iris. They were gone now.

We were two new people on a journey together.

CHAPTER 11

The streets vibrated with the chatter of voices and the rush of people weaving in and out of one another, looking get to their destination a millisecond faster than the previous day.

Iris and I made our way from the safehouse and swiftly stepped out into the tide of commuters, being swept along like an inexperienced swimmer caught in a rip current. I had studied the map of the area and memorised where we needed to go the night before, so it was a case of Iris and I getting from Point A to Point B without being detected by the Security Forces.

It was the busiest part of the day and we knew it would give us the best chance to get from where we were to where we needed to go. The current of people would help us blend in and, unless you knew who or what you were looking for, you would not be able to tell us apart from the many faces and bodies that streamed through the streets.

Iris and I looked completely different. No one would recognise her at all from the photographs that The Authorities were surely circulating amongst themselves. My haircut, skin colour and contact lenses were able to change me well enough that I should have been able to slip through any nets cast by those wishing to catch us, but the change in my appearance could never have been as dramatic as Iris'.

On street corners, there were Security Forces dotted around with their usual red and black uniforms and faceless helmets. The helmets had smart glass that scanned the crowds for known criminals and people who were wanted for questioning, so Iris and I were incredibly nervous as we made our way to the Metro station, no more than five minutes away from the safehouse.

Iris held my hand tightly. It was as though that connection between us was a lifeline that she was unable to let go of, even if she wanted to. If she were to have let go, it would have been as though an umbilical cord had been cut and she would have lost all food, blood and oxygen.

I was so proud of her. As she walked, I knew that

she was nervous as the grip on my hand tightened and loosened as we neared Security Forces or security cameras. On the outside, she looked totally calm, breathing deeply and doing her utmost to keep her eyes fixed on the sign of the train station so as not to attract the attention of stray gazes and looks.

Every pair of eyes were landmines to her. She knew if she made eye contact with the wrong person, we could both be caught and that would be the end of everything. The end of me, the end of The Resistance and she knew she would be disappeared into some basement in the middle of nowhere, never to see the light of day again.

The world she had seen and experienced in the short time she had been freed from The Institute was enough to make her not want to return. The feeling of the Sun on her skin, the feeling that fresh air gave her as it cascaded into her lungs and cooled her from the inside out and the attachment she had to others around her, myself and Dr Rosen. All of these things were like giving a blind person back their sight, a deaf person back their hearing or a paralysed person the ability to walk again. To Iris, I could tell that the world she had been introduced to was worth not being caught.

The stairs to the Metro system opened up ahead of us and sank down into the pavement. Commuters streamed up and down the steps with the same impatience that the rest had. Iris slipped in behind me, still holding my hand, as we descended the stairs. I gently squeezed her hand to let her know it was all ok. We had made it from the open and into the enclosed walls of the Metro system.

The distant, dull roar of the Metro trains could be heard below us and the heat of the stale trapped air rose up and hit us in the face. It tasted bitter, like the breath of the thousands of people who exhaled down there earlier that morning and the morning before that.

We stood on platform six and waited for the train to Hexingham North. The pre-purchased tickets Seth had given us were clenched safely in my right hand as we waited for the train to pull up.

We only had six minutes to wait, but they were the longest six minutes of my life up to that point. The spaces beside us on the platform filled up rapidly as more people squeezed in to find a spot on the train that was soon to pull up. The closer the strangers got to Iris, the more nervous she began to feel. She was not used to this invasion of personal space. The people around her were only making their way to a chosen destination but, to Iris, it was claustrophobic.

It wasn't long before one of them brushed up against her and looked at her, almost apologetically, but this worried Iris. She pulled closer into my side and squeezed my hand tightly.

I turned to the man who brushed her and half-smiled at him in acknowledgement of his half-apology. I leant down to Iris and whispered, "It's okay. You're doing great," into her ear. She smiled nervously and snuggled into me, like a little sister would to her elder sibling in a strange place that was as busy as the Metro station was.

The man beside us nodded acceptingly at the look I gave him, and he turned to look down the tunnel in search of the train that was still four minutes away.

The whole world seemed to grow more impatient as the years passed. There was a time, when I was a girl, that people would help others and be warm to each other. Now, times had changed, and The Authorities liked it that way.

The Authorities liked the fact that everyone was untrusting, unaccepting and unwilling to help each other. This meant that they had everyone turning one eye towards each other, looking for anything out of the ordinary, while the other eye turned a blind eye to the obvious lies and hidden truths that were in plain sight.

The new world was selfish, self-obsessed and secularised. No one wanted to know about anyone else's problems and this was the cycle and mentality that The Resistance wanted to shatter once and for all.

The hope was that Iris was the brick to start the revolution and rekindle some kind of humanity inside the hearts and minds of a population who had grown desensitised and apathetic.

Two minutes remained on the train timer.

To my left, I noticed three members of the Security Forces making their way down the stairs with automatic weapons in their hands. Their glossy black, faceless masks were scanning the crowd, almost robotically, looking for someone of interest.

I directed my eyes to look left while moving my head as little as possible, so as not to attract attention to Iris and I. The three of them continued scanning the crowd until one of them studied a data screen on his forearm, surely double checking the identity of who they were looking for.

I kept my head looking forward and did all I could to hide my discovery from Iris as she rested her still sleepy head on my arm, while wrapping her arms around mine.

My heart pounded in my chest. I was surprised Iris couldn't feel my hammering pulse as the blood was pumped furiously through my arm as she clung onto it.

Suddenly, the Security Forces' attention was alerted to something in our direction. I could hear a discussion between the officers that I couldn't fully make out, but I heard the dreaded words, 'over there'. The three officers slowly cut their way through the commuters packed onto the platform.

One minute remained until the train arrived.

The crowd slowly began to part between us and the three officers. I had convinced myself that I could hear their radio chatter, describing us and that they were to take us alive if possible.

Behind us, an agitated man started to move away from the officers and towards a flight of stairs and the exit. "Move! Move!" he ordered as he worked his way through the crowd.

The officers quickened up their pace to pursue the man as he fled. It was then that I heard the security officer talk. "The suspect is exiting on foot towards the southern exit. Have Alpha team pick him before we lose him, again!"

The three officers made their way through the crowd and after their suspect, as the lights of the train appeared out of the darkness of the tunnel, like a shining light of a saviour coming to rescue us from those who wished to do us harm.

As zero minutes ticked onto the timer, the train pulled up, the doors opened and Iris and I stepped into the carriage to find seats. With each step I took, my heartbeat calmed, and my breathing deepened, in through my nose and out through my mouth.

The carriage filled rapidly and very soon the doors closed and the Metro train pulled away from the platform, into the next black tunnel that swallowed us whole, like a predator eating its prey.

"I'm sleepy," yawned Iris.

"Close your eyes and rest. I'll wake you when it's our stop."

I never told Iris about the Security Forces that day, or how close I came to pulling her by the arm and running as fast as the packed crowds would allow us to. There was no point in telling her.

Nothing happened.

We sat on the train and Iris closed her eyes to sleep, with her head resting on my shoulder. Slowly, my overheated imagination started to tick itself cool and gradually return to some sort of equilibrium and normality. My mind started to think clearly again and return to the plan that had all been set out before us.

Just before the train disappeared into the tunnel, I saw the Security Forces trailing a beaten and bloodied suspect across the platform towards the other stairs. His arms were in restraints behind his back and his head hung helplessly from his shoulders.

He was crying.

I was relieved it wasn't us.

CHAPTER 12

The train cut silently through the tunnels and Iris slept the whole time. Every so often we stopped at a station and commuters hopped off and on, almost as though the train was inhaling and exhaling – breathing to recover from its journey between stations.

The faces of people came and went, stop after stop, station after station. Iris and I appeared to be the only immovable objects, sat silently on their seats. Every other seat was only there as a stopgap for people to perch momentarily as they waited for the voice to announce that their stop was coming up, like birds perched on a wire above the city resting before flying off again.

I looked down at Iris' face as she slept. The only movement was that of her chest rising and falling.

She was exhausted.

I expected nothing else considering her entire world was being turned upside down. Everything she thought she knew about the world was being shown to her in a different light. Memories she had were starting to return with the lower doses of drugs, people she knew from the past were beginning to return, like ghosts in a séance, almost from the dead.

The world she knew was metamorphizing, like a butterfly from a cocoon – she was only beginning to spread her wings.

Under her eyelids, I could see her pupils dance and move from side to side – she was dreaming. I found myself deep in thought about what she may be dreaming about. Were they the first dreams she could consciously remember? Were they welcome or were they nightmares? Was she dreaming of me, Dr Rosen, or something completely unconnected from what she had lived through the past few days?

A lady sat down opposite us with a red handbag. She was dressed in clothes that were dark, dull and totally nondescript. In fact, no matter how hard I try to remember them, my memory sticks on the red handbag.

She sat opposite us and nodded at me, smiling a half-smile in acknowledgement that I was there. I returned the gesture and continued to scan the now almost vacant carriage.

"She looks exhausted," the lady stated, to the point.

"Yes, she was up early this morning and didn't get much sleep," I replied, trying my best not to get involved in anything resembling an in-depth conversation.

"Sisters?"

I nodded in reply and smiled politely, hoping the questioning would stop soon.

"I could tell," she replied. "You look so alike." The more she talked, the more I was drawn to the bright red lipstick as her lips moved, revealing perfectly white teeth.

I lifted my phone from my pocket and pretended I was looking at it, with the hope that this lady would stop talking or the voice would announce that her station was up next.

"She is so pretty you know." I tried my best to avoid question, but the lady had a look about her that made me think she would not tire easily.

"Thank you," I said. "Everyone says we look alike. They say we get our looks from our mother." I searched around in my mind for something, anything

I felt would bring this conversation to a close. All I could think about, was what would happen if this lady recognised me or Iris. Would she report us? Would she help us? I was unsure. All I knew, was that I did not want to take chance. Iris was too important – she was everything and I could not risk losing her. "She died when we were young."

"Oh, I'm so sorry! I didn't mean to…"

"It's okay," I replied, "it happened many years ago and my sister and I have dealt with it, but it is still not a subject that she likes to talk about."

"Absolutely! I totally understand! I didn't mean to pry," she apologised, looking genuinely annoyed that she had managed to bring up a subject so personal in such a public place.

We sat quietly for a few minutes. Another station came and went, and the train pulled away from the platform and on to its final stop. The lady with the red handbag, Iris and I were the only passengers left in the carriage.

The silence that hung in the air was palpable. With every heartbeat, it felt as though the air vibrated, causing a ripple that reverberated through the carriage, like the ripples on a pond when a pebble broke its surface.

"The disguises are truly excellent," the lady said, taking me totally by surprise.

I was taken by surprise and was unsure how to reply to the sudden statement made by the lady in red. "I'm sorry?"

"You don't need to worry, I have something for you." She reached into her red handbag and lifted out what looked like a phone and left it in the tiny space between the two seats opposite us. It was then that she took her handbag, stood up and went to leave. "Annyagh is remarkable at what she does. Don't worry, no one will recognise you." With that, the lady with the red handbag walked down to the end of the carriage and went into the restroom.

A voice came from the speakers above to tell us that our stop was the next one, and the end of the line. I shook Iris to wake her and stood up to retrieve the phone from between seats opposite us.

I sat down beside Iris again and looked at the phone. Iris stirred and rubbed her eyes to help wake herself up. "What's that?" she asked.

Just as she finished asking the question, the phone rang. On the screen, the number and said was 'withheld'. Instantly, my stomach did a flip and I felt sick. Who could this be? How did they get this number? And why did they want to talk to me?

I answered.

The voice on the other side of the phone was encrypted. Someone had taken care to distort the voice to ensure that they would not be recognised. "Good morning, Jade, it is wonderful to finally talk to you."

"Is it?" I asked.

"I know you're probably wondering who this is, and whether you can trust me or not. The truth is you simply have to trust me even though you don't know me.

"I promise you that all will become clear in time but, at the minute, all I need you to do is get off the train, exit the station and make your way to the taxi with the red circle sticker on the back window. I have arranged for the transport to take you to your next destination, where you and Iris will begin the next leg of your journey."

I was speechless, unsure of what to do and I knew that, if I made the wrong choices, I could endanger not only my life, but that of Iris as well.

"I know Iris trusts you and I know you will do a great job looking after her. Think of me as a friend or a guardian. It is my job to look after the both of you.

"We have a lot of work to do, and that work starts now. I look forward to finally meeting you. Stay safe and I will meet you in time."

The phone hung up and the train came to a halt. I took Iris' hand and stood up to exit the train.

"Who was that?" asked Iris.

I wondered what I could say. Too much would scare her, but I informed her that I was speaking to someone who was trying to help us. "He was our guardian," I replied, doing my best to reassure a girl when I wasn't sure myself.

We stepped off the train and made our way to what I hoped was safety and a road to freedom.

CHAPTER 13

Just as the distorted voice promised on the phone, the taxi with the red spot on the window sat outside the station. We loaded our bags into the boot and got into the back of the taxi.

The driver was a middle-aged man who said little, if anything. It was obvious that he had been given an address to take us to as we did not have to give him a destination. He simply drove off, weaving his way through the traffic and on towards the city limits.

I always loved driving my way from the city into the countryside. It was as though I was leaving civilisation behind and escaping into what I thought was a pure way of life – a way of life that was still somewhat untouched by the filthy hand of corruption in the larger cities in the country.

Behind me was the chaos, the control and the

overarching authority that seemed to want to know our every move. A place where security cameras and Security Forces were on every street corner, where people were stopped, searched and asked to provide proof of identification just because they didn't quite fit in with the rest of the worker bees in the hive.

The countryside was obviously not completely free of that but, at least here, we would not feel like we had to look over our shoulders every second of the day. It wasn't as if I was naïve to think that the Security Forces would not try to find us outside the larger cities, that much was inevitable, but at least we could breathe a little, even if it was only for a short time.

In the fields outside, hills rose and fell like salmon rushing upstream. On the fields, marked out with hedges and fences that crisscrossed the landscape like the marks of a sidewinder snake across the desert floor, hundreds of white clouds munched on grass, passing the time as the Sun warmed their young as they lay at their feet.

Before long, the taxi pulled into a long gravel driveway. The crunch of the stones under the tyres was the only noise we could hear. Iris sat silently, almost transfixed by the surroundings she had seen as she made her way through the countryside for the previous hour.

Iris had lived all her known life in The Institute and probably had few, if any, memories of what had come before, so the sweeping hills, green fields and what remained of the woodlands that surrounded Hexingham probably came across as something new to her.

The taxi pulled up in front of a house that I had never seen before. It was well hidden from the road by tall trees and it looked as though it had been owned by someone with lots of money as the grounds were too large and too well maintained for someone to look after it themselves. The house itself was obviously well looked after by people who were paid to keep it that way.

We got out of the taxi and the driver helped us get our bags from the boot. He carried on to the door and swiped a card on a panel on the wall and the door popped open.

We walked in and left our bags in the hallway and as I turned to talk to the driver, was already on his way out the front door.

"Where are you going?" I asked.

"Do you have the phone?" he asked.

"It's in my pocket."

"He will call you. Just make yourself at home and do not leave the grounds of the house."

"Is that it?" I asked, wanting to know if any help was coming.

The driver stood silently for a few seconds, his face without emotion. "He will call." And with those words, he left, and the door closed behind him with the click as the lock engaged.

The entrance hall was beautiful. The floor was covered with an expensive-looking cream tile and the staircase that stretched up from one floor to the next was a rich oak that all looked as though they had been polished freshly for our arrival.

On the walls, there were no pictures of people or family members. Instead, there hung pieces of landscape art of mountains, lakes and other areas of natural beauty. They were the type of pictures that were so detailed you swore you could actually step inside them, smelling the scents of flowers, fresh air and feeling the breeze as it gently kissed the skin on your face.

Iris and I went into the kitchen to see what there was to eat. The kitchen was a contrast to the entrance hall. Where it looked classical and matched the house, the kitchen was sleek and modern. All of the worktops were white polished stone and the appliances were all state of the art. It made me think that the person who owned the house rarely cooked and preferred to ask the oven to cook the food to perfection instead of actually do it themselves.

I went to the fridge to get some food. There was an abundance on every shelf. It was obvious that someone had loaded the fridge just before we arrived, as the food was well within date. I lifted some sandwich meat, bread and some chilled water with glasses and Iris and I ate.

All we could do was sit and wait for the phone call to come. The more I stared at the phone, the more I felt it was mocking me, teasing me that my whole life appeared to revolve around it. For that time, that piece of plastic, glass and metal was the centre of my universe.

After we ate, Iris and I went off to one of the bedrooms to give Iris her medication. She had been great when taking all of what Dr Rosen had given her but last time she took it, she felt nauseous and I was worried that she would refuse to take the medication if I was not there to administer it for her.

Dr Rosen had set out all the doses for me to

administer until Iris could be weaned off onto a weaker medication. I knew that with his guidance I was in no danger of making Iris overdose or fall ill.

"Do I really have to?" she asked, like every other teenager or child who had ever been asked to take a medicine they didn't like.

When I was a young girl, I remember my parents used to make me take cod liver oil capsules. I knew they didn't taste like fish, but because I hated fish with a passion, I would feel I was going to vomit if I swallowed them. When my parents gave me the huge capsule to take, I would work it under my tongue until they left me in the kitchen and I would spit it into the waste unit – a machine that turned everything fed into it to a brown mush that was collected and used as compost.

Iris was so like me that it scared me sometimes.

"You know the answer to that question. I promise it will be easier. The more you take it, the easier it will get. Dr Rosen would never do anything to hurt you, you know that."

"I know. I just…"

"You can sleep it off. Once you take it, I will lie with you until you fall asleep. If you sleep off sickness, it won't be as bad as last time. I promise." I never liked making promises I had even the slightest idea may not have been true, but I knew that Iris needed to be reassured more than being fully aware of the facts.

Iris took the medication without complaining and curled up in bed, leaving just enough space for me to lay down beside her. She rested her head on my chest and breathed slowly and deeply, doing her utmost to relax herself and take her mind off the nausea that was surely not far off setting in.

"You relax me you know?"

"Really?" I asked, unable to hide my surprise, considering most other people in my life usually said the opposite.

"I love listening to your heartbeat. When I breathe slowly and deeply, listening to its beat slows mine down too."

I loved hearing Iris say those things to me. It made me feel warm inside and reaffirmed my belief that I had made the right choice in joining The Resistance, leaving my life behind and putting myself in danger for a cause that was bigger than myself. This girl, who was curled up relaxed and helpless beside me, relied on me to protect her, to care for her and, if required, give my life for her.

The longer we lay there, the slower her breathing became and eventually her body went limp and she drifted off to sleep.

As I pulled away from her and pulled the blanket around her to keep her warm, my pocket buzzed as the promised call finally came. The number was withheld again but I knew that it was the distorted voice from earlier, probably calling to check that we had not left the grounds of the house.

I left Iris in the room, closed the door quietly and made my way downstairs before I answered the call just in case I woke Iris from the sleep that I knew she surely needed.

"You're still alive," the voice remarked, almost teasing me.

"Did you expect anything else?"

"Of course not. Our friend in the taxi would not have allowed anything to happen to you. I pay him too much, trust me."

"Trust you? How am I supposed to trust you? I don't know you. You won't even let me hear your proper voice. If you want to build some trust, even a little, let me hear your voice – your real voice."

"And that would build trust?" asked the voice, still

dripping with distortion from the mod he was using to mask his identity.

"It would be a start."

"You do realise I can't do that, don't you?"

"Why not?" I asked, trying my best not to let my anger show. For all I knew, this man could report our location to The Authorities. We were truly at his mercy. If we decided to step a foot out of line, he could drop us like a stone – or at least me, having his 'taxi man' take Iris and leave me somewhere without a heartbeat or able to take a breath.

"You have no idea who I am, you have no idea of the connections I have, and you have no idea what they would do to you, Iris and I if they were to find out where she was or if I had anything to do with her disappearance."

"So you are one of them then?"

"Of course. Did you really think you and The Resistance could really have gotten into The Institute without my help? Who do think the security guard was on the gate? How do you think you got your pass? How do you think you got the encryption software to control their cameras, alarms and anything else you wanted to control? It was all me – me and the 'taxi man'."

"Does the 'taxi man' have a name?" I asked, trying to glean any information I possibly could.

"Of course."

"You're not going to tell me it, are you?"

"Of course not," he replied, using what was swiftly becoming a catchphrase, almost a habit, uncontrollable – like Tourette's syndrome. "I live and work in a world where giving away the slightest piece of information could lead to your death.

"Our friend in the taxi, is in charge of all of my security, in fact he is listening into this call right now. He is a very skilled man with a lot of experience and I do exactly as he tells me to. If he tells me not to tell you anything, I will not tell you anything.

"Everything we have done and are going to do is depending on my secrecy, at least until the time comes when I must reveal myself."

"When will that be?"

"When the time comes. You really don't listen very well, do you?"

Inside, my anger started to bubble, boil and almost boil over. I bit my tongue and imagined I was talking to a very secretive source from my journalism days. He may not have been able to reveal anything about himself, but I also knew that if I were to reveal my own anger it would be a sign of weakness, of lack of control and could ultimately put us all in danger.

"So is there a plan to all of this?"

"All of what?"

"To Iris? This house? Me watching over her? Dr Rosen? Any of this?"

"Of course. Do you think I would endanger my livelihood, my standing and ultimately my life for there not to be a plan?"

I didn't answer.

"I'm glad you agree. I have arranged for a visitor to call with you tomorrow. He is someone you already know, and I feel it best that he call to check Iris over."

"Dr Rosen?"

"Yes. He knows her better than anyone. The Resistance and I would feel much more contented if we knew that she was fit and healthy. Well, as healthy as can be considering the circumstances."

"At least I will see a familiar face instead of wondering if I am able to trust any of these strangers who seem to appear out of the woodwork."

"Strangers? My darling, we are all friends here. We

are a brotherhood and a sisterhood. We are all fighting for the same cause. No one within The Resistance is a stranger to you. We are all family."

"I have never had family who use voice scramblers or refuse to let me know their name."

"Is a name what you want?"

"It would help."

"Call me The Benefactor," and with that the phone line went dead.

CHAPTER 14

I was unable to sleep a wink that night. Outside, the wind howled, and heavy rain pattered almost ferociously on the window and the roof. I lay on my back and stared at the ceiling, my mind constantly wandering between the multitude of events that had taken place in the past few days.

The Benefactor's voice was stuck in my head. The tone of the voice scrambler, the fact he called me 'darling' and those dreaded words, 'of course' that drove me insane every time. I heard them playing in my head all night, through the distortion of the scrambler.

In a way, I understood why he was unable to break his anonymity and risk his safety. After all, from what I had heard and investigated about The Authorities when you crossed them, I wouldn't want to share my identity with too many people I didn't know. Even if they were part of The Resistance – the sisterhood and brotherhood.

In the next room, I heard Iris shuffle around in her bed, moaning and groaning as though I was not the only one having a restless night. I got out of bed and made my way into her room to check if she was okay.

The bedsheets were kicked off her and onto the floor and her arms and face were glistening with sweat. Any part of her body that was uncovered looked like it has been sprayed with early morning dew or even frost on a winter's morning.

I swiftly went over to check her temperature in case she was burning up as a reaction to the drugs Dr Rosen had prescribed for her. When I felt her forehead, she was not burning up. Her body temperature was normal.

I turned to go back into my room to get my phone to call Dr Rosen but as I reached the door I heard Iris talk.

She is so peaceful.

This isn't right, you know?

I do, but what else can we do?

She's only a girl.

Iris is the key to everything.

So you keep saying.

If this cure works, if it really works, it could save millions of people.

Does that make what we're doing right here, doctor?

I'm afraid not, my dear. If I could change things, I would.

I slid the sheets back over Iris and her body immediately started to relax, as though she had managed to exorcise the inner demons that were preying on her mind. Iris then rolled over onto her side and started to sleep once more.

The room fell into silence.

I made my way into my room and got my phone to call Dr Rosen. I sat at the desk, facing out towards the open countryside, the dim glow of Hexingham lighting up the night, like a post-apocalyptic scene of a metropolis burning down to the ground, leaving nothing but ashes and rubble.

I had never thought I would get a glimpse into Iris' subconscious so soon. I was unsure whether to share any of this with Dr Rosen, considering that it was clear he was one of the people in the conversation that Iris was relaying.

I started to wonder what would happen if Dr

Rosen reacted negatively to what Iris let me see. If he deserted us, whether it be out of shame or any other multitude of feelings he could be pressing down deep inside himself, what would happen to Iris if we needed him in an emergency? I knew Dr Rosen was extremely conflicted about everything to do with Iris and The Institute so I was torn between telling him right away and holding off to see if any other information came to light from the shadows behind Iris' eyes.

The phone rang and was picked up almost instantly. "Jade? Is everything okay?" answered Dr Rosen.

CHAPTER 15

I sat down with Dr Rosen at the table in the kitchen, setting his coffee in front of him as he stared out of the window. The noise of the cup making contact with the glass table interrupted him from his trance as he traced imaginary lines with his mind, like a dot-to-dot scene, between livestock or the land and sky above.

"Thank you, my dear," he replied in his extremely polite and professional manner. There was never a time when Dr Rosen addressed me that he didn't use the same courteous tone.

"She is okay then?" I asked, still somewhat shocked at the episode that had played out the night before in Iris' bedroom.

"Yes, it is a normal side effect of the medication and her withdrawal. Unfortunately, there is nothing much more we can do." Dr Rosen looked down at the coffee cup, took a sip and looked back up into my eyes. "I'm sorry for what I am putting you through."

There was a silence in the air. It hung weightless and unmoving, like a helium balloon floating in the air on a day with hardly a breeze to move it. Unavoidably, this silence, this balloon attracted the attention of both of us, no matter how hard we tried not to look at it.

"If I had stood up to those above me, asking me to carry out the research in the first place, maybe events would have taken a different path."

"How can you be so sure?"

Dr Rosen paused, almost taking a breath to prepare him for the information he was about to divulge to me, like a free diver before submerging himself underwater. "My research was the conductor, the catalyst for everything that is happening right now. I am the Genesis.

"At the prime of my career, the world was changing. Everything I got into medicine to do, everything that inspired me to be the person I had become was changing too. Some out of necessity and some out of something else – something altogether more sinister.

"I was charged with looking after Iris when she was brought to us. She was a tiny waif of a thing with blonde hair, elven features and bright, shining silver eyes.

"I had read her file and knew everything there was to know about her. One thing about me is that I am thorough. I cross every 't' and dot every 'i' right down to the most minute detail, but I wasn't prepared for how I would feel when I saw that little girl standing before me.

"She was like a doll." Dr Rosen paused, taking a moment to compose himself. It was obvious that the conversation we were having was awkward for him, but I also felt that he needed it – a cathartic moment to cleanse him of his guilt and wrongdoing.

"I held out my hand and she looked quizzically at me. This was understandable being in a strange place with strange people and, most importantly, alone without her parents. I knelt down in front of her and looked her in the eyes. They were majestic.

"I introduced myself to her. I told her my name was Dr Wilhelm Rosen and I had been asked to look after her. She looked at me, still unmoved. I told her there were lots of people in The Institute – some older people and some younger, like her. They had lots of other people to look after them, but she was special. I told her I was there to look after her and only her.

"Those words stirred something in her and she finally spoke. Her first words to me were used to say her name wasn't Iris, but instead her name was Annabelle.

"I smiled at her. She had an innocence about her that was palpable." Dr Rosen paused again. Every time he paused, it was obvious that he was feeling guilt or shame for what he had done at The Institute. "I replied to her, telling her I knew that her name was Annabelle, but there, in the special place, we were going to give her a special name. There, her special name was Iris. She looked at me through her brow.

"I told her it was like a nickname. She smiled and replied sweetly, telling me she'd never had a nickname before. I felt as though she was warming ever so slightly to me.

"I smiled and stood up, holding out my hand. I asked her if she would like to go see her room. Iris stood silently, looking up at me with her glistening eyes. Without saying a thing, she eventually took her first tentative steps towards me, took my hand and walked down the corridor towards her room.

"Her hands were so small. They felt incredibly soft and as cold as ice. Her other hand was up to her mouth and she was sucking on her thumb while her eyes scanned everything around her – taking it all in.

"That was the most nervous I have ever been in my life. When I walked down that corridor to Iris' room, I knew the weight of the world was on my shoulders – literally.

"She was the key to everything and, as far as I knew, her health, safety and well-being was in my hands. Everything that passed her lips and was injected or retracted from her was up to me.

"In the beginning, at least."

"It wasn't like you were doing all of this of your own accord, Dr Rosen," I interjected, trying to make the man see that he was not totally the evil demon he was making himself out to be.

Instead of replying, he smiled narrowly, enough to acknowledge the point that I tried to make. He continued, "Time flew by. The initial months were simply used to gather more information to confirm what we found out in the initial tests – she was the perfect candidate. Everything about her was what we needed to conduct all future research.

"Any time we tested her DNA against the known

viruses or diseases, it seemed to slow their growth or, in some cases, totally eradicate them. I knew that it was only a matter of time before we could synthesise Iris' DNA and refine our processes and the results we initially had would be even more successful.

"It was only a matter of time before the diseases and viruses Iris' DNA only slowed would be defeated."

"It is a lot of pressure to put onto the shoulders and body of someone so young, so fragile," I replied, unable to stop myself from voicing my feelings about the fact that Iris was having all of this done to her at such a young age.

"Iris was, and still is, the key to everything. She is our future." Dr Rosen's tone changed.

For the first and only time I felt he was almost defending his work. It was obvious from talking to him and looking into his eyes that he was a tortured soul. It was clear that he wanted desperately to feel awful and hate himself for what he had done to Iris in The Institute, but it was also obvious that if the human race was to eradicate the coming diseases and epidemics that were warned to be on the horizon for all of us, something had to be done.

Iris was the key to it all.

"When I had spare time, Iris would ask me to come play chess with her. She and I would sit in her room at the table in the corner, in front of the artificial view of the artificial garden from her artificial window and play for the hour or so I had for lunch.

"Most of the time, I wouldn't eat. My wife always made such huge breakfasts that I would rarely need a lunch. A coffee would suffice most days and Iris and I would strategically try to plot each other's downfall. We rarely finished a game but, if that was the case, I would leave her to study the board and, sure enough, the next afternoon she would have plotted out the next moves and I would usually find her saying the words, 'Check mate.'

"There was no doubt that Iris was a hyper-intelligent girl, but it wasn't that she was just simply intellectual, she was also so incredibly sensitive and emotionally tuned into those whom she was in close contact with.

"The longer I spent with Iris, the more I started to see Elaina, my own daughter, in her. This is where I started to have a conflict of interest with the programme The Institute ran with Iris.

"The successes we had in the first few years with Iris and the conditions she helped us treat or cure started to slow, and the decision was taken to step up the work that we were doing.

"It wasn't long before we were drugging Iris to keep her somewhat sedated throughout the day and, at times, even putting her under anaesthetic to perform more intrusive harvesting of cells and tissues.

"I voiced my concerns with the powers above me and was told to do my job, so I did – and it killed me inside.

"I remember coming into the room with the chessboard after a month or so that the sedation programme had been running and Iris had wholly changed. She had gone. The girl before me was a shell who had been reduced to no more than a lab rat and it was all my fault.

"I would go home in the evenings and feel that I couldn't tell all to Stefana, my wife, I was scared of what the Authorities would do to us if I spoke out about the treatment that was going on in The Institute. They would kill us, so I kept my mouth shut and kept on with the programme, not telling Stefana anything until I couldn't bare it any longer.

"When I returned home to find her face down on the floor, it was the worst day of my life. I tried to help her, but I knew it was too late. She was gone,"

Dr Rosen started to weep. He took out a handkerchief from his pocket and wiped his eyes to free them from the tears that were gathering.

I felt so sorry for the man. It was clear that he was doing his utmost to escape from the system he had been a part of. He wanted to repent, but that wasn't enough. It was though she was struck down by some overarching, all powerful deity who was hell bent on making a point.

"The hospital said it was a massive heart attack and she had died no more than an hour after I left for work that day. When I finally told her everything and she knew I was unhappy, I knew she was worried about the effect that my job was having on my health. I just didn't expect it to kill her.

"It should have been me," those words were weighted with sorrow and intent. It was clear that Dr Rosen meant every one of the five words. He must have looked at himself every morning and considered the fact that he believed those words to be true.

"I had to leave the Institute and retire. I couldn't take it anymore. The treatment I was carrying out on Iris had sunk her deep into some recess in the pit of her consciousness, my own conscience was shot to pieces and my wife had been taken from me. I had to go.

'I remember the retirement party. All of the higher

powers were there praising the work I had done for 'humanity'. That made me laugh. Humane? Us? We were anything but.

"My colleagues all stood up and gave glowing speeches about the successes I had in my career and how I was a beacon in my profession – a guiding light that led them to follow in my footsteps. I felt ill. In the pit of my stomach, I knew I had to get up to make a speech soon but the glowing words my fellow professionals were sharing about me were rushing over me, like a tide, and I was drowning.

"What did they see in me that I could not? If I did see anything of it, I hated it – I was a demon.

"I heard my name called out by the host for the evening, Dr Rasmus, the new head of research at The Institute, and I got up to make my way to the stage and the microphone atop of the podium. I fumbled in my pocket for the scraps of words I scribbled down on pages the night before.

"The applause around me was muted, muffled and distorted in my head. People like those around me wished and longed for evenings like that, and I did too earlier in my career, but at that moment I couldn't enjoy it. Every step I took was leaden and every breath I took was tainted and tasted bitter. The faces of those colleagues around me distorted and twisted from the faces of those I knew and, in some way still respected, into something that wasn't human.

"When I stood on the podium and said, 'Thank you,' the room quietened, and everyone sat back into their seats and looked up at me, with bated breath, for words of wisdom – anything that could help give them some validation and comfort that they were on the right path, serving a noble cause that would one day eradicate most if not all disease and illness. All so sure of themselves but craving the recognition of fellow peers.

"The speech I had written was one last chance to receive praise from those around me for the years of work I had done and all that I had achieved. On the other hand, it was a resignation that I was walking away from Iris. I was leaving her alone to face all that I knew was ahead of her but that she had no idea was even on the horizon.

"I spoke to the room, pretending to be the person, the caricature, that I had allowed myself to become. I was disgusted with myself, but I knew that if I refused to paint the picture The Authorities wanted me to, I would be disappeared.

"I scanned the room from right to left, making eye

contact with those whom I had retained even the slightest modicum of respect for. I still had some dear friends in my profession, even if I didn't agree with their morality or values when it came to the work they were now pursuing. Slowly, one by one, they were all turning their backs on the oaths they had taken when they first started in their professions and were moving into a world where anything went when it came to medical research.

"As I looked around the room, mouthing the meaningless words, I couldn't help but consider whether I was the person who was in the wrong. Maybe we were supposed to abandon our beliefs and values when crises came around, but I couldn't.

"As soon as those thoughts rose in my mind I automatically saw Iris and was swayed back to my original decision being the correct one – to leave and deal with my conscience when I met my maker.

"I always carry the speech I made that evening in my pocket. I see it as a constant reminder of what I was and what I swore I would never become again." Dr Rosen took the folded-up paper from the breast pocket of his coat and handed it to me.

The note was written with italic font and it was clear to see that the note was written with attention to detail and pride, as though he refused to let Stefana's death go in vain.

I read the note:

I leave this profession in a place much richer and full of promise than that which I had joined all those years ago. We are entering a time of such wonder and advancement that I could never have imagined as a young man.

You, my fellow colleagues, possess a hunger and desire to evolve us, to make us stronger and become all that we were meant to be. We have everything in our hands to make the leap to the next level of human existence so use those hands to heal us, to nurture us and to raise us up as a civilisation onto a higher plateau than we have ever been before.

"Those were the final words I shared with my colleagues and the room erupted into deafening applause as I took my bow.

"The baton was passed on to the next generation and I was meandering my way through claps, slaps on the back and handshakes into obscurity while the rest scrambled towards the light."

Iris appeared at the kitchen door. "I'm hungry," she said.

CHAPTER 16

Iris ate like I'd never seen her eat before. Dr Rosen and I stood in the doorway of the kitchen and watched Iris as she looked out intently at the livestock meandering across the field of the farmer's land behind the house.

"This is normal," Dr Rosen whispered to me as he watched Iris closely. "Iris' body is slowly starting to react against the drugs she got at The Institute. The medication we… they gave her would suppress any appetite she had outside of the food she was given, either by intravenous means or the meals that were left to her at specific times. Iris would never actually feel hunger properly because we wouldn't let her. We fed her when she needed fed, simply to keep her alive and healthy – like a lab rat." When Dr Rosen said this, comparing Iris to a lab rat, his voice sank, and he was ashamed of himself.

He loved this girl and he realised that he made her into nothing more than a commodity – something that could be used and reused until it was no longer needed, or it could be sold off for whatever value was left in it.

"She really lived something that barely resembled an existence, didn't she?"

Dr Rosen didn't acknowledge this. His silence was more of an affirmation than he could have given me by nodding or even speaking words he felt were suitable to reply with.

The fact was, he couldn't speak – he was ashamed.

"For the first time in years, she is experiencing hunger and appetite," he continued. "Before, when you fed her, you gave her meals as I instructed you, is that right?"

"Of course," I replied, tutting at the fact The Benefactor's Tourette's was rubbing off on me. I almost found myself tutting in disgust that I was resorting to using those words. It was like they were now engrained into me, like lettering in a stick of rock.

"Now you will notice that she will eat of her own accord and, for a short while at least, she will eat what seems to you like a lot, but that is normal. She will return to a more acceptable level of eating in a few days."

We just stood there watching Iris eat round after round of toast. She must have had at least six rounds of toast and showed no sign of slowing soon.

As far as I could see, I would have had no problem letting Iris eat whatever she wanted and however much she wanted, within reason. The girl's brain was most likely firing off chemicals, like fireworks on Halloween or the fourth of July. Every sense that was being plucked within Iris was beginning to make music – a song that was precious to her but that she had not heard for a long time.

"The next stages of the medication will start to counteract more and more of the sedatives she was given at The Institute and she will start to act and be more like a 'normal' person. She will be less monotoned and less robotic at times." Dr Rosen was always so frank and to the point when explaining anything linked to Iris' treatment or past. "You may see some mood swings and irritation issues arise as she starts to engage with her emotions for the first time in years. You will have to show extreme patience and understanding with her."

"I will, don't worry."

"I will go and discuss the next step of the treatment with Iris before we talk, just so she knows what she is going to be feeling and how she may be able to control the issues that come up in the coming days and weeks." Dr Rosen walked off towards Iris. He put his arm around her and rested his hand on her shoulder before sitting down on the chair beside her.

When I saw Dr Rosen, it was obvious that he was someone who cared about Iris when she was at The Institute and now that she was back in his care for a second time, he wanted to make amends for any pain he had caused her.

This was Dr Rosen's repentance. He would not allow himself to make the same mistakes a second time. Mistakes were supposed to be opportunities for us to learn and make changes to our actions or our characters. Dr Rosen was an incredibly analytical mind and I had no doubt that he was continually scanning his actions when he was last caring for Iris to check he was indeed walking a different path, even if it was a longer, winding road with many dangers underfoot.

I stood at the window of the front room – a sitting room with tables and chairs that looked as though they had barely been sat on. The room had a smell of disinfectant, but it was obvious that it had not been used much. I came to the conclusion that The Benefactor must have had the house deep cleaned before we arrived and, if he was as careful as I thought he was, he probably had the whole house swept for surveillance devices.

The Benefactor sounded like another man who would cross every 't' and dot every 'i' just to ensure there was no chance of him being exposed as the mole who helped free Iris.

The world around *us* was incredibly cloak and dagger, so the world The Benefactor lived in and the circles he moved through were sure to be littered with Judases, thieves and backstabbing, two-faced friends who would undoubtedly do all they could to usurp your throne and feed you to the wolves if it meant stepping up one more rung on the ladder.

Part of me was incredibly frustrated by the fact that he would not tell me a name or let me hear his voice without the distortion, but I also had to respect the man for the care he had taken.

Surely, the lengths he had gone to ensure Iris and I got away unharmed and the fact that he had arranged for two safehouses already showed that he could be trusted.

I knew then that my sceptical, investigative mind was the flaw, not The Benefactor. This was something I would need to work on if I were to fully accept being in an organisation like The Resistance where we would have to trust others with our very lives.

I just hoped it wouldn't be too long until I met him and could read him in person.

Outside the front of the house, a young deer stood nibbling on the wildflowers in the forest just beside the house. The deer nibbled at the flowers, carefree and peacefully, like it was exploring some new surroundings it had not come across before. Testing the waters with the tip of a toe just to ensure it was safe enough to enter.

Its lean, vulnerable body stood arched over the white flowers as it bent down to pick the heads off. Periodically, it lifted its head to check for any predators or voyeurs, like me breathing in the beauty of such a timid young creature in the wild. Across its tan fur, there were lots of white spots, like stars pockmarking the night sky. They highlighted the body of the deer perfectly. Even though these markings could help those hunting it, they also showed off an exquisite colouring that only the finest of artists could recreate.

Outside the window was the canvas of a master and I was stood, like an ignorant admirer, who barely understood any of the splendour before her.

"Would you like to come in, so we can discuss the next steps?" Dr Rosen asked from the doorway behind me. I didn't even hear him approach me. I knew I needed to sleep and, if Iris was to sleep again later that day, I would have to rest too. I would have been no use to her if something serious happened while in the state I was in.

I followed Dr Rosen into the kitchen again and sat with him and Iris at the table, looking out over the fields behind the house.

"How are you feeling?" I asked Iris who had finally stopped eating and sipped at a glass of chilled water.

"I'm tired but I don't want to lie in bed anymore. I feel like I'm back in that place," she replied frankly. I couldn't blame her. Between myself, Dr Rosen and the doctors at The Institute, she had slept for what had seemed like an eternity. She *needed* to rest but the last thing she wanted to do was rest.

Iris needed to live, at least as much as she could within the confines of safehouses until we got her to safety.

"We can rest down here," I replied. "We can lie down on the settees and rest if we want to. No one is making you go to bed now, Iris."

Dr Rosen interjected, "I have to stress that you are entering a very important but testing time, Iris, so rest is important, but I agree that you need to take advantage of being away from The Institute. Just promise me that you will rest if you feel tired."

"I promise, I will."

Dr Rosen continued, "The stage you are at now will be tough on your body. You will feel like you have much more energy and you will feel less tired than you did before, but this energy will quickly lapse, and you can crash if you aren't careful."

"I will look after her, Dr Rosen, don't worry."

"You will also start to feel things you have rarely felt before. Things like emotions, hunger and tiredness. When you were at The Institute, you were fed at certain times, were sedated by injections and your emotions were supressed by taking pills every morning.

"From now on, we will use less of all of this medication and you will feel the effects. The hard thing for you will be recognising when you are frustrated, angry and nervous. You may cry at things that would not previously have upset you."

"Did I not feel *anything* before," Iris asked, almost disgusted with herself at the fact that she could not remember.

"Not really. We could not allow you to feel too much in case you rebelled against what we were doing, or it affected the results of certain tests we were carrying out.

"Emotions can affect you physically and, according to those above me, we could not let that happen." Dr Rosen looked away from Iris and his eyes fell onto the table, almost in recognition of the fact that Iris was hurt by this admission. "You were too important. We couldn't let anything endanger the research."

"Even allowing me to feel?"

There was a silence as Dr Rosen looked up and into Iris' eyes again. The shimmering glint of silver pierced Dr Rosen right to his soul.

"I am sorry, my dear."

A single tear welled up and meandered down Iris' cheek. Both Dr Rosen and I watched as it sped up and slowed, tracing the contours of Iris' beautiful, doll-like face.

Iris did not wipe it away. She knew it was there.

She felt it as it tickled the almost translucent hairs on her cheek, but she refused to remove it. That tear was a badge of honour for her and she wore it with pride.

"Will I ever know what they did to me?"

"Possibly, some day," Dr Rosen replied. "You are too young to know this now. When you are older, if I am still… I will tell you everything, I promise you."

As I sat there, the third wheel in this exchange, I found it interesting that Iris never once referred to Dr Rosen as being someone responsible for the lack of feeling, emotion or even the experiments that were carried out on her.

It was as though, somewhere deep down inside Iris' consciousness, she remembered Dr Rosen, and some of the experiences she had with him in The Institute. I couldn't help but wonder whether she *knew* he wasn't responsible for all that happened to her and that all of the orders were passed down to him by people on high.

This was something that I had to battle with at the time. I knew that Dr Rosen was in charge of the research institute, but I also knew that he answered to people above him. Very persuasive people. Very dangerous people. The kind of people who would make your life misery if you dared cross them.

That's if they let you live at all.

Dr Rosen reached across the table and held Iris' hand. His eyes were pink with tears and an obvious bottled up torrent of emotion that he was doing his utmost to shield from Iris and I.

"What are Iris and I to do now?" I asked, desperately trying to move on and get some answers about what was to happen in the days and weeks ahead.

Dr Rosen let go of Iris' hand and continued, "The Benefactor is arranging safehouses and protection for you with The Courier."

"The Courier?"

"The gentleman who brought you here." In my mind, I screamed at the frustration that another one of these people whom we were to trust and put our life in the hands of refused to share an actual name with us. "They will contact you in the coming days with a time of collection and you will be brought to the next destination."

"Where is the final destination?"

"I do not know. As far as I am aware, The Benefactor will arrange this with you and you alone. Only when you arrive at the destination, will he contact Seth and share this information."

"So, no one knows we are here other than you, Seth and The Benefactor?" I asked, seeking clarification and security that we were not completely exposed and being hunted down by The Authorities. I knew that every organisation could have leaks and The Resistance was no different. In my head, I imagined the Security Forces infiltrating Bethlehem and someone letting slip where our location was.

"That is correct," Dr Rosen replied in his professional, matter-of-fact tone. "This is all to ensure your complete and total safety. Seth does not want anyone to know your whereabouts in case The Authorities have a spy within The Resistance. Now that we have Iris, we don't want her location to be exposed."

"I understand."

Iris stood up and made her way to the back door that led to a large decked area with chairs and a table. She closed the door behind her and curled up on one of the seats. I felt it was a moment of realisation that her energy levels were starting to flag.

"She is strong, you know." I looked back at Dr Rosen and his eyes were fixed on the back of Iris' head. "Once all of this treatment is over, you will see a different side to her. She may look like a fragile waif of a girl who would crumble as swiftly as you look at her, but I know what is inside of her."

"How do you mean?" I asked.

Dr Rosen looked deep into my eyes. "The future of humanity."

CHAPTER 17

I joined Iris out on the chairs. She had not moved since Dr Rosen had left but wore a look of utter determination across her face that she would *not* sleep. Even if it meant that she just sat there and stared at a fixed point a mile away in the distance, she wanted to stay awake, constantly absorbing all that was around her and inside of her.

For all I knew, she could be physically tired, but her brain would be frantically firing and fizzing, like a chemical reaction burning itself away, creating something beautiful but distrustful in the process.

Who was I to make her sleep? She deserved a chance to explore the world she had found herself in.

"What are you thinking?" I asked, studying the expressions on her face to see if she let out any clues that would hint to an answer.

"Everything," she replied. I was unsure whether to press further with this reply, but Iris answered that for me. "I feel as though I have been asleep for an eternity. It is as though someone has brought me back to life, like some creature made up of body parts from a dozen different people who have lived a dozen different lives."

Iris paused, gathering her thoughts, trying to create an understanding out of the explosions of sparks in her brain. I could only imagine it was like an inexperienced soldier fighting his way through a chaotic battlefield. With explosions deafening him and launching pieces of earth tens of feet into the air, screams and shouts of differing urgency and in differing languages all while trying to stick to a strategy some military genius gave you before you engaged the enemy.

Iris was in a battle, doing her utmost to get through no-man's-land and pass to the other side – whatever the other side was.

"In my head, I remember things, but the memories I have don't feel like they belong to me."

"Tell me something you remember."

Iris closed her eyes and started to speak, visualising the memory as it played out on the back of her eyelids, like a movie being screened for the first time in years. "I remember Dr Rosen reading to me. He is sitting on a chair beside my bed and I can see him, but I can't move. When he reads, his voice echoes, but I can make out the words. He reads about a doctor who creates a creature and, when the creature wakes up, it jolts to life and its eye opens for the first time. I remember he read about how the doctor felt about the creature – he called it an abomination and a demon."

Iris stopped, her eyes still shut, eyelids flickering with the effort of remembering the memory in such detail. When she opened her eyes, her eyes were pink from the effort of recalling the memory and the emotion she was undoubtedly feeling.

"I feel like that creature. I feel like I have the fragments of twelve people's memories patched together, like a collage, in my brain. I feel like an abomination." She paused again. "I feel like a demon. Like I don't belong."

At this point, I stood up and sat beside Iris on the chair. I held her tight into my chest and kissed her on the head. Her body was trembling slightly, like a newborn foal experiencing the world for the first time – cold, timid, anxious and excited. "You are *not* a demon or an abomination. Do you hear me?"

Iris stayed silent, staring off at the same spot she was earlier. Did she see something that I didn't or that I wasn't privy to? Was she able to see through a portal, into another world, where she saw herself living a normal life, with a normal home, in a normal house with her parents? Was it that, or was it simply because she had nothing to say?

"You are free now and will soon understand just how important you are. I know you have a million things running around your head right now, but we are all here to help you. I am here to help you." I sat Iris up and cupped her face in my hands. "You are my world now, you know?"

She smiled slightly, both eyes now streaming with tears.

"Wherever you go, I will go."

"I don't even know who I am," she said, her voice full of anguish and sadness. Feeling lost in a world as messed up as the one Iris found herself in was bound to make her anxious and terrify her, especially as she didn't remember anything of who she was.

"We will learn who you are, together," I said, as reassuringly as I could, knowing that this girl was going through torment.

"How long will it take for me to remember?"

"It will take as long as it takes, Iris. The memories will come when they are ready and, when they are, we will talk about them and try to piece everything together."

"But you weren't there either. How will you know?"

"We have Dr Rosen, remember. He was there, and he will be able to place events a lot better than anyone." This seemed to appease Iris a little and she lay her head on my chest. As she lay there, heart still pounding, I stroked her hair and hushed her to try and relax her.

On his way out, Dr Rosen reiterated the importance of calming Iris down when she was upset and, from what he saw, the relationship she had with me was akin to that of a younger sister and her elder sibling. He knew that she trusted me and that I was patient with her – the most valuable trait to have during this time.

"Be patient and listen, those are the most important things you can do, Jade," he said as he stepped out the door. Before he left, he turned and hugged me. "You have a kind heart, my girl. Show it to Annabelle. You will show her more love and kindness than anyone else has her entire life."

"Annabelle what?"

"I'm afraid I cannot tell you that. Not yet anyway. We need to focus on what is important and that is ensuring that Iris is kept safe and is nursed through this time ahead." He inputted his number into the burner phone. "If ever you need me, any time of the day or night, call me on this number. I can come and sedate her if needed, but I would prefer that she recovers without the use of sedatives. They will only set us back and Iris' recovery will take longer."

Dr Rosen left into the afternoon Sun and I made my way to Iris – Annabelle.

As I sat holding Iris, she eventually drifted over to sleep, something she was determined to fight off, but I was relieved to see her give in. I slid out from beneath her resting head and went to get the burner phone from the drawer in the kitchen.

Doctor. It's Charlotte. Erica had a slight emotional episode. She is okay and resting. I hoped I could get some files to read – help piece some of the puzzle together as she shares. Would you have anything you could share? Thanks. Charlotte P.

When texting Dr Rosen, I thought it best to use the aliases we had all agreed upon just in case The Authorities were scanning the communications networks for words, like Iris, Institute, Dr Rosen, Resistance and even my own name.

I was doing my utmost to cover all bases.

I knew I had excellent research skills as a journalist and I knew if Dr Rosen could get some files for me to read I could try to piece some sort of timeline together out of the fragments that Iris gave me.

When it happened, who was there, why it happened and possibly even how. I knew I would not be able to place memories like the Frankenstein one that Iris had just shared with me before I sent the message to Dr Rosen but, with his help, I knew I would be able to piece together some of the private interactions between him and Iris. Working together was the only way to totally piece together everything that happened.

I sat at the kitchen table and used a notepad to jot down all of the details that Iris told me before she slept. I figured it would be a good place to start next time Dr Rosen came around to check up on how Iris' progress was going.

As I paused to recollect what Iris told me, I looked out at the swaddled up sleeping girl on the chair outside. Her face was peaceful, like it always was when she slept.

I just wondered what horrors may lurk deep within her mind and how they may manifest themselves as the treatment went on and the beasts became unleashed.

CHAPTER 18

"Wake up, Iris," I said, quietly, as I woke her from her sleep. She breathed in a deep breath and stretched as she woke. The imprint of the pattern on the arm of the settee that was etched into the side of her face showed just how well she slept and how much she needed it. "How do you feel? Any better?"

"Did I sleep long?"

"A few hours," I replied, keeping the fact that she slept for six hours to myself, "but you needed it, so don't worry."

"I always feel so tired," Iris spoke, while yawning. "It doesn't seem to matter how much I sleep, I always seem to need more."

"Dr Rosen said it would be like this, remember that."

"I know."

"You have to be patient."

Iris smiled slightly in recognition but not fully in agreement. "It's so quiet here. I didn't like the city. Everything was so busy. People rushing from place to place, from here to there, not caring how they got there or who they walked through to get there.

"Those days were like watching ants in a jar as I sat looking out the window. I know I was locked in that place but, from what I could see, those people were just as trapped as I was."

Iris seemed to have an amazing insight and could see things within people that others could not. She had experienced very little of the outside world other than what she had lived before she went into The Institute. She would ask what objects were and want to know how they worked because everything was done for her in The Institute, but she could read people as though they were transparent panes of glass and see right into their soul – right into the heart of their beings and see what made them tick.

I knew by looking at her that she was continuously doing the same to me. She was always analysing my movements and gestures. I knew this, but I didn't mind. I had nothing to hide from Iris. In fact, I liked that she was reading me so intently because then she would be able to see that I was genuine and that she could trust me completely.

It would also mean that she would be able to study and analyse strangers that we may come across. If I were to miss something, the fact that she would be able to have an insight and an opinion on the person's true intentions would mean that she would help me keep both of us safe.

We sat silently together on the settee outside. Iris lay into my side and we wrapped a blanket over us as the evening air started to chill. Suddenly, I was back in my back garden as a little girl, allowing the cold to creep up my body from my extremities.

In the distance, the Sun was waning down towards the horizon and the night sky slowly started to invade the azure blue that preceded it, turning the blue to deep blackness that went on for infinity. The night sky was spoiled by the far-off glow of Hexingham – the city of fallen angels who set up their heathen kingdom below the heavens they were expelled from.

Those expelled would surely have tried their utmost to recreate their own version of heaven but, no matter how hard they would try, their attempts failed. The earthly representation of paradise would inevitably turn in to Hell, a Hades that we on Earth would have to suffer.

"Why me?" Iris asked, her eyes fixed on a distant star, almost asking a god to provide her with an answer. To spell it out to her in the form of a shooting star tracing across the sky above.

"I can't answer that, Iris," I replied, answering her as truthfully as I could. I wasn't there to provide answers to things that I did not know. That was the job of Dr Rosen. Iris trusted me, and I did not want to do anything to jeopardise that trust.

"Just over there, in that city, I know that there are so many people looking for me. They are knocking on doors, asking people questions and stopping cars to see if I am there, but why? Why not someone else? Why did I have to lose my life while everyone else lives theirs?"

Iris never took her eyes off the star in the sky the whole time she was speaking to me. I was unsure if she even wanted me to provide an answer. I never had the heart to tell her that, yes, The Authorities would be looking for her, but they would be doing more than knocking on doors and asking questions. Many lives would be changing forever that night as we sat under the stars and stared off into the distance.

People would be taken from their loved ones, questions *would* be asked but more forcefully than Iris would even think.

"You are special, Iris, in more ways than you know. I don't know all the details of why you were chosen and not someone else, but we will find out together. Dr Rosen is the key and we will answer those questions one by one."

Soon, Iris' breathing slowed and grew deeper. Her body went limp and she was asleep again.

I held onto her and slowly started to drift off into something that resembled sleep myself. The calm noise of the breeze toying with the leaves on the trees and the distant sound of cars travelling down the road beside the house helped me to drift to sleep. The sound of the tyres on the road sounded like a parent shushing their child to sleep.

My eyelids felt leaden and my breathing slowed, taking deep, long breaths that opened every part of my lungs to the chilled night-time air. It was the type of air that felt and tasted new. Virginal air that had been untainted, never breathed in or out before.

"No," Iris moaned, shuffling in her sleep against me just enough to stir me from the dream that was beginning to materialise in my mind. "Don't do this again, please."

Iris settled again, briefly.

"You promised I would never have to take the medicine again." She paused as I sat up, allowing her head to rest on my lap. "Please, it burns my stomach."

Suddenly Iris lurched in her sleep and clenched her stomach tightly. "Ow, it hurts." Iris started to relax and fall back into her sleep. "Why are you doing this to... me?"

Iris' body went limp again. I stroked her hair and kissed her on the forehead to soothe her. There was a tiny film of sweat gathered in microbeads across her forehead. It was cold as my lips made contact with her and tasted salty.

As I pulled away, Iris started to whisper in her sleep.

Is she under?

Yes, she should be.

This has to work, the contract is worth too much for this to fail again, Rosen.

You don't need to tell me how important this is.

Just make it work.

Do you ever think about how this is a little girl we are subjecting to all of this...?

Just do your job. Remember who you work for.

FP-17 is almost cured. I'm sure this will work.

It better.

Iris' body went limp again and her breathing went back to normal. I stood up and carried her inside to the large settee in the living area and lay her down. Being built so fine, it meant that Iris wasn't impossible for me to lift. If anything, it made me remember just how she was fed only what they needed to give her to keep her healthy enough for their tests to be a success.

I took the burner phone and went out onto the decked area again and called Dr Rosen. The phone rang for no more than five seconds before it was picked up.

"Charlotte, is everything well?" he asked in a concerned tone.

"Erica is well, but she had a dream and I think we should discuss it in person when you bring the puzzle round tomorrow."

"Ah yes, surely. I have all the pieces of the puzzle in a box ready to go. I took a while to find some of the pieces but all that I have is there for us to make a complete picture. Is Erica resting?"

"Yes, she's down."

"Rest is all she needs right now. I will bring some drinks with me tomorrow. A different flavour may help her sleep, something more soothing. You know?"

"I do."

"I will see you tomorrow as planned."

"I look forward to working on the puzzle with you."

"It will be a challenge, my dear Charlotte. Lots of tiny pieces to put together."

"I love puzzles," I replied and hung up the call. I put the phone into my pocket and went inside the house again.

After locking the door for the night, I turned to look at Iris as she slept. She looked so peaceful as she rested. I walked to the breakfast bar and sat down with my book to write down all of the details from Iris' dream. Everything from the whispering voice, Dr Rosen's name and that he was talking to an unnamed person. I finished by adding the key piece of information that could help us to track down the file and find out exactly what was done to Iris and who was present in the room – 'FP-17'.

CHAPTER 19

Those first few days were tough. I was glad to have Dr Rosen with us. He arrived, as promised, the next day and brought a tablet computer with him, containing all the files he had for us to piece together the dreams Iris was having. He also carried a black medical bag with all of the medication Iris would need through the coming days or weeks, however long Iris needed to flush the remaining sedatives and drugs out of her system.

Every morning, afternoon or evening it was as though we could have a different person enter the room. Both Dr Rosen and I would get up early and sit in the kitchen at the breakfast bar to get our own food before Iris rose. This preplanning was the only way we could ensure we had everything we may need to calm or even sedate Iris if needed.

Each morning, Dr Rosen had a syringe of each variation of sedative beside him under a clean drying cloth, just in case we didn't have time to draw the medication out of the bottle before injecting it into the young girl. I always felt uneasy preparing like this, but I trusted Dr Rosen and his experience of dealing with patients like Iris. After all, he was there to help her, not set her back further.

Iris' good days were amazing. She would come down from her room, share breakfast with us at the table and talk endlessly about her dreams and flashbacks.

When she had days like this we would record what she said and go through the files that Dr Rosen had brought with him and look for patterns and matches to see if these events were things that actually happened, they were figments of her imagination or they were hallucinations brought on by the fevers she took due to the detox programme she was on.

Dr Rosen said that some of the come-downs from the medication could bring on fevers and give Iris dreams that felt so real that she would swear they were actual memories. These 'memories' would not necessarily have been from her time in The Institute. They could even have been from the previous day and she would swear that events took place that hadn't happened.

Iris would then have days that were not so good. These bad days would consist of various things, like extreme mood swings, depression, nausea and sometimes serious fevers where Dr Rosen would have to step in and administer any medication Iris may have needed.

These days were the hardest. I would feel powerless to help other than to hold Iris down or pin her to a wall while Dr Rosen injected her with some sedative that would cause her to go almost totally limp and we would have to carry her to the settee or her bed and let her sleep it off.

These days broke my heart.

I would be constantly beating myself up in my head, constantly wondering whether what we were doing to this girl was right. Were we just as bad as the people in The Institute? Were we adding to the situation? Was what we were doing to Iris detrimental to her health?

The worst mood swing I remember Iris having was one where she started off trying to recall a flashback from the night before and she wasn't able to see it clearly enough in her own mind. She jumped up from the table and smashed her glass off the wall beside us.

Dr Rosen and I did what we could to try and talk Iris down, explaining to her that her memory would stutter and stall when recalling memories that may have happened many years before. We tried to say that we would have found it hard recalling memories that far back and that was without being sedated for so long and trying to remember things from the mind of a very young child.

Trying to calm her down wasn't good enough. She saw everything I said as an insult or a slight on her. The next thing I knew was I had a chair flying towards me from across the table and it smashed straight through the sliding glass doors that led out onto the decking. When the loud smash cut through the air, it appeared to snap Iris out of her mood and she collapsed onto the floor in floods in tears.

It was only a matter of minutes before she was calm again and was apologising for doing what she did. She also begged me to call The Benefactor, so she could explain and apologise to him for smashing his window.

I called The Benefactor while Dr Rosen brushed up the shattered glass and put it into the bin, but he just laughed and said The Courier would be around to replace the glass in a few hours and, like he said, The Courier arrived with workmen and had the window fixed in no time.

Iris was hiding upstairs, keeping herself out of sight as best as possible. I knew this was the best place for her, not just to hide her from any eyes that may have recognised her but also because I knew I would have been mortified if I had workmen come around to replace a glass door in my parents' house when I was her age.

When I went up to get her, she was sobbing. Her face was wet, puffy and red from crying so much. She apologised over and over, telling me that Dr Rosen and I must hate her for all of the trouble she was causing us.

I held her hand and told her she was to say nothing more of it and come back downstairs. We would not talk about any more memories that day and would do nothing more than play board games and listen to music.

The thought of her being in charge of the music was enough to make her smile and laugh as she wiped away the tears from her cheeks.

That was enough to calm her down and get her to

come back and join us downstairs.

The worst day I can remember was when Iris took a serious fever that was refusing to break. Dr Rosen stayed by her bedside from morning to night, constantly monitoring her temperature.

Dr Rosen tried everything he could to bring down her temperature and heart rate, but he didn't want to use any of the old drugs Iris was on as she had done so well to come off them over the weeks we were at the safehouse.

Just after midnight, Iris' temperature was extremely high, and she was flailing around as though she was possessed during an exorcism.

This was the scariest thing I had ever witnessed, and it affected me for a long time afterwards. I would try to sleep at night and wake with a start, thinking I could hear Iris having another episode. I would jump out of bed and rush to the room, only to find her fast asleep and lying in complete silence.

It had all been in my head.

Dr Rosen and I held her down while we discussed whether to give her a dose of her strongest medication again, just to settle her down. This was a battle for both of us as we knew that she had made such progress without any of her medication, but was this the time we had to take one step back to make enough progress that it got her through the detox programme? What did it matter if it was a few days later than we had first hoped? As long as Iris made it through the programme and was healthy was paramount to us both.

We both agreed to give her the sedative and Dr Rosen lifted out the bottle and syringe to draw the dose. I held Iris down as best I could, pinning her wrists down while sitting on her hips.

Dr Rosen lined up the needle, ready to inject but, just as he was about to insert the needle, Iris settled, and she collapsed down silently onto her bed.

Dr Rosen couldn't believe it.

We both sat down on the edge of the bed and watched this young girl's body return to something that resembled normality.

Dr Rosen disposed of the medication and fell back into the seat beside Iris' bed. The man's shirt was soaked through with sweat and he was panting, probably with a mixture of exhaustion and relief at the fact that Iris' temperature was starting to come down.

After Dr Rosen was happy that Iris was on the mend, he went back to bed. I went into Iris' room and curled up beside her. I didn't sleep, I couldn't if I wanted to. Instead, I lay awake all night, stroking Iris' hair, letting her know I was there for her, no matter what.

CHAPTER 20

I woke up the next morning to find Dr Rosen sitting drinking coffee at the kitchen table. The smell of coffee filled the air and gave it a texture, a thickness that reminded me of home and that the day was about to begin.

As a child, my father always brewed fresh coffee and had to have at least two cups before leaving for work. My mother would then have at least one cup herself before taking me to school.

Those days were pleasant memories to relive and visit from time to time. The smell of coffee first thing in the morning was a welcome trigger to revive memories long since been and gone.

"Your notes are intriguing, my dear," Dr Rosen commented as he read a page of notes from my notepad while sipping on his dark, black coffee.

"I tried to get down what I could just after any episodes she had. Sometimes I would have to wait until she slept or was up in her room, so I apologise if there is anything that I missed."

"No, please, don't apologise. You have done a splendid job with Iris and these notes will help piece together what she has seen and where the memories have come from."

I poured myself a cup of coffee and made my way over to the table to join Dr Rosen. "Have you been up long?"

"Only an hour or so," he replied, not taking his eyes off the page. "I truly hope Iris sleeps until later. She needs the rest, but it will also give us some time to look at these records without her asking questions."

"We aren't going to keep this from her, are we?"

"Some of it, I'm afraid we will have to, simply because it could cause too much upset for her at this time. There is some of it, on the other hand, that we will be able to share and give her some of the answers she is craving."

"She needs to know what she was exposed to, doctor," I said firmly, not able to hide my protective urges towards Iris.

"Oh, I absolutely agree, but just not all of it right now. Iris is still in a sensitive state and it could set her back some distance. I think that, when she is older and able to understand the complexities of the situations, she will be able to learn everything."

"I see. She has been through too much and deserves to know what happened during her time in there."

"These files are yours to keep once I am gone and you can share them with her when you feel she is old and mature enough to deal with the information within them."

I nodded and took the files from across the table. The tablet computer lit up and I was able to scroll through some of the folders and information held within them.

Dr Rosen studied me from time to time through the tops of his glasses, seeing if I was reacting to anything that I was reading.

Some of the folders were named after Iris with a date after them but others were more cryptic – FP-17, Norallia, Strossa Syndrome, Llorassum and HX7.

"Some of these folders have odd names," I said to Dr Rosen, hoping that he would elaborate.

Dr Rosen took off his glasses and held his coffee in two hands. I had the feeling that he was bracing himself for the plethora of questions that I was bound to ask.

Like a Pandora's Box, he wouldn't be able to put the information back once I'd seen what was inside.

"Those are diseases, conditions and syndromes that we used Iris to cure or ease," he answered, sipping on his coffee once he was done. "It's like I told you," he continued, "I understood that what we were doing in The Institute was necessary, but I was ashamed of how we were going about getting our successes and how far we were having to go to achieve them."

"How can you say that what you were doing was necessary? You were torturing her," I retorted, sharply.

"Not at the beginning." Dr Rosen sipped at his coffee again and leant forward to rest his elbows on the table. "Some of the research we started with was simply done by using saliva swabs, taking a little of her blood or even using hairs from the hair brush in her room.

"What you have to understand here, Jade, is that the beginning was beautiful."

Dr Rosen hung his head and sighed. He was

toiling with inner demons and guilt that no one knew. I knew that I would never learn everything about what made this man tick or what happened in his past. I also knew that he would keep some things from us, things he didn't want anyone to know, but I owed it to Iris to get what I could from him while he was with us.

"At the start, Jade, Iris was able to do much of what any child her age would. We let her out into the garden, she would play and once a week she would even have a 'treat night' where we would let her watch a movie and have some popcorn and a drink.

"When we heard of the Norallia outbreak in India and Pakistan, the World Health Organisation declared it an epidemic and were worried it could spread to other countries.

"People were vomiting, unable to eat, suffering from dehydration and becoming so weak that they would die. We were able to get sent a sample of some infected people's blood and once it was mixed with just a few drops of Iris' blood, the disease subsided.

"We were able to make cures from Iris' DNA and send it to the areas affected.

"Within weeks, the epidemic was reduced to nothing."

"So, you were helping people?" I asked.

"Yes! The work we were doing in the beginning was magical. We had never seen anything like this before. It was exciting."

"What about FP-17?"

Dr Rosen sipped at his coffee and peered into the bottom of his cup, as though searching for an answer to the question that would be somewhat more palatable. "This was the start of my... dissent and... disenchantment with my role within The Institute.

"A new board was put in charge of The Institute and instead of simply trying to cure diseases and conditions for the good of humanity, this board wanted to try and maximise profits over the care of Iris and the other patients we had in our care."

"There were others?"

"Yes. We had five 'subjects' altogether and used them for varying research. Iris was by far the most successful. Inside her there was electricity, a special spark, a genesis of something that we could utilise to save people, Jade. Not just a few people but millions of people.

"But these people who came in to run the research above me weren't interested in that. They would cure diseases and conditions but only for a price."

"Was all of the work done to save people?"

Dr Rosen laughed into himself. "At the start, yes, but not always when the others were in charge."

"Some of the research was for cosmetic use, like skin toning and hair loss."

"So, you're saying rich people could buy the 'cures' your team were researching just to satisfy their own vanity," I replied, finding it hard to hide my disgust.

"I'm afraid so, my dear. I remember using strands of Iris' hair to synthesis a tonic that could be used to rub on the heads of bald men to help hair grow. It just so happened that one of the executives on the board was as bald as an egg."

"I suppose he offered himself forward as a guinea pig to test it for you?"

Dr Rosen laughed. "Yes, you are right, Jade, indeed he did."

"Did it work?"

"Why, of course," Dr Rosen exclaimed, opening his arms wide to emphasise his success. "It was a huge success! Bald men were practically falling over themselves to buy the stuff!"

I couldn't help but laugh at how pathetic the

whole situation had become. Dr Rosen had started off fighting disease and was then made to find cures for the baldness and sagging skin of rich people who clearly didn't know or even want to know where the ointments and tonics were coming from. "I can't believe it."

"It's ridiculous, my dear. I remember when I was called in to the board meeting to discuss marketing this tonic to the public. I simply sat there watching the executive, with his now full head of hair, go through just now lucrative this tonic could be. 'Billions,' he said. When he got into the numbers of how much profit could be made, he predicted The Institute could make over a billion pounds a year for the next five years.

"Once he said that, the board started to explore other ways to sell 'cures' to the mass population.

"After that meeting, I went down to my office and started planning how I was going to leave the profession I had given my life to."

"Is the man that Iris spoke about in her dream one of the board members who pressured you?"

There was a short pause before he replied, "You are correct. His name is Malcom Barton.

"When the FP-17 disease started to spread, it

started to cross borders in Africa. The problem with FP-17 was that it infected drinking water, almost like cholera.

"Once it started to take hold, the doctors in the area tried using cholera medicines to treat the patients but, instead of reducing their symptoms, it made them worse and, unfortunately, the patients deteriorated rapidly and died."

"That's awful."

"Mother Nature can be a wonderful, caring person but she can also test us at times. It's like Darwin's theory, 'It is not the strongest of the species that survives, nor the most intelligent that survives. It is the one that is most adaptable to change.' Mother Nature challenges us to adapt, to evolve and to become more than we were before."

"But if we are curing diseases, are we not cheating Mother Nature?" I asked.

"Exactly, we are, Jade. Every time we cure one strain of a disease, it mutates and comes back ever so slightly different, and sometimes many people die. This was the case with FP-17."

"How did you combat it?"

"We tried using some of Iris' saliva that we

gathered using swabs, but it was ineffective when the doctors administered it out in Africa. In the lab, we have positive results but, when the vaccine was sent to the infected patients, something went wrong."

"What happened?"

Dr Rosen paused, setting his coffee cup down on the table. "People died. Lots of people died.

"We still don't know what it was that caused the reaction, but Malcom was livid. He came to me in my office and screamed at me, telling me that those people's deaths were on my head and that The Institute would have to refund part of the contract if the next vaccine didn't work."

"What did you do?" I asked, seeing that Dr Rosen was getting upset. It was clear that the incident with FP-17 affected him. It cut right to the core of his being. He was a man who cared greatly for humanity and dedicated his life to helping people so, when his vaccine caused deaths instead of reducing them, a part of him must surely have died inside.

"What could I do? Malcom was right, I had caused those people's deaths. It was on me and I was ashamed of myself.

"I went straight back to the data and looked at the research using the saliva. I kept thinking that we must have missed something, but we didn't. We had covered every possible angle and the results were a success in the laboratory.

"Still, to this day, I carry that with me and it still bothers me what it was that caused that vaccine to fail.

"The next day, Malcom came to me and suggested we operated on Iris and extract matter from her stomach.

"I felt uneasy with this and made that clear to Malcom, but he didn't care. He told me to prep Iris for surgery and 'do my job'. So, I did. We got Iris ready for surgery and the conversation Iris recounted in her sleep is the exact conversation Malcom had with me as he stood over my shoulder, watching me perform the operation."

"Did it work?"

"Yes, this time it was a success and The Institute didn't have to refund any of the payment it had received when the contract was agreed with the World Health Organisation. But FP-17 had taken its toll on Central Africa. Over five million people had died in the outbreak and some of those dead were because I missed something."

"From what you have said, you did everything you

could, Dr Rosen," I said reassuringly.

"I did, but that still doesn't bring back the fifty thousand people who died after taking my vaccine. It still doesn't take back the fact that I broke a promise to myself, Stefana and to Iris, that I would never do something I felt was unethical and that I disagreed with. I would never cross that line, but I did.

"After that, I planned my resignation with Stefana. It's just a pity that she didn't get to see me see it through. The last thing she saw of her husband was that man who broke a promise to a little girl."

Dr Rosen got up and left the table.

I sat there, with the tablet computer in front of me, skimming through file after file to see what else Dr Rosen and his team did to Iris after the FP-17 outbreak.

CHAPTER 21

That day was one of the first that Iris hadn't had an episode or felt completely drained with exhaustion. The change in her demeanour and her personality was like night and day.

The new Iris entered the kitchen, as Dr Rosen and I sat at the table, saying, "Morning," in a bright, almost musical tone.

As soon as Dr Rosen and I heard her greeting we turned around, almost expecting to see someone else, an imposter, but Iris walked swiftly, as though she glided across the floor, barely gracing it with the soles of her feet, and went straight to the fridge to get herself breakfast.

Dr Rosen and I turned back to each other and smiled. He lifted his coffee cup to his mouth and gave me a comforting wink so as to tell me that we had turned a corner. In that one gesture, Dr Rosen was able to assuage my worries, my anxieties and doubts over the treatments Iris was going through.

He had, in that one wink of an eye, fully affirmed to me that he was a man of his word and had come full circle. From the man who loathed himself and felt he had made a deal with the Devil all those years ago when allowing his standards to slip and conduct tests that he felt were morally wrong, he had finally expressed penitence for his actions.

It was as though I saw a weight leave his shoulders, disconnecting itself from his earthly body and drifting away into the Otherworld, where exorcised inner demons, fears, regrets and shame passed when they no longer tortured the souls of those that they previously inhabited.

Before Iris came down, Dr Rosen and I had discussed what was in some of the files on the tablet computer. Some of the information was very trivial and didn't really warrant discussing in more detail, like Iris getting a flu that had been passed to her by one of the nurses and a test had to be delayed by two weeks until she was treated, and it was out of her system – to ensure the data and results gleaned from the test weren't affected.

What came out most in the files that we read through was the discontent of Dr Rosen and some of the other staff members who appeared to disagree with the testing that was going on at The Institute.

In some of the files, Dr Rosen's notes were very plain, boring and simply pointed out the facts of what the results were and whether they were a success or failure. "You can see the difference, can't you, my dear?" Dr Rosen asked as I scanned the notes, comparing them between the early days of testing and the latter.

"Why are they so different? It's like the earlier notes are written by a completely different person," I replied, pausing to look at Dr Rosen, reading his expression as I did so. "Anyone could have written the later notes. They're... soulless."

"That's exactly it, Jade. You read people so well! That is a skill that I hope you can instil in Iris as she grows up and becomes a young lady.

"In the earlier notes, you can see how alive I am. I am full of electricity, charged and ready to take on the world. Every day, I felt like I had a 'Eureka' moment and could run through the corridors screaming my successes to everyone and anyone who would listen to me.

"The latter days were different. You are exactly right, my dear, I was soulless. The Institute had stripped me of everything that had made me Wilhelm Rosen – my life, my verve… my humanity."

I looked at him as he almost hung his head, drawing invisible shapes on the table top with his index finger, almost signing a confession. "You are not that man anymore, Wilhelm." I took his hand in mine and he looked up at me. He was not looking for reassurance but, as he said, I could read people very well and he was not Dr Rosen of The Institute anymore – he was Wilhelm Rosen of The Resistance, the man who helped free Iris. "They may have killed the man you once were, but now you have done the same with the man they created, the man you had become when at The Institute.

"Look at me," I commanded as he hung his head once more. Wilhelm looked up at me through his brow, like a schoolboy being scolded by his teacher. "You freed Iris! You freed her from The Institute, you freed her from Hexingham, you freed her from those horrible thoughts and feelings she was having when she was trying to find herself again in the world outside The Institute."

I paused, staring straight into Wilhelm's inner

being, mining deep into his core. "You have been resurrected, Wilhelm. Do you hear me?"

Dr Rosen nodded ever so slightly, showing that he understood what I said. Whether he believed it or not was another matter. I knew he would not see it right away. It could have taken him months or even years to see even the smallest shred of decency in himself after all of this was over, but the first step is always the most difficult to take.

Iris came over to join us, breakfast in hand. She was in such high spirits. It was as though the dreams and discussion about her feeling so low about herself the night before hadn't happened.

I loved seeing her laugh. We sat outside on the decked area; she and Dr Rosen talked about a pet he had when he was young, a German Shepherd called Bruno, who would terrorise his parents and the neighbours in the local neighbourhood.

"He was such a loyal creature, Iris," he shared. "No matter where I went, he followed. If I was ever to stray too far from home, Bruno would lead me back. If someone was to pick on me or make me feel threatened, Bruno would simply growl quietly and show his teeth and the bully would leave me be.

"I loved him, and I knew that if anything was to

happen to me, that dog would have my back and protect me from harm."

"Like you and Jade with me?"

"Exactly right," I added, smiling at Iris before sipping at my cup of coffee.

"Bruno had bad habits though. I remember my father bought a brand-new pair of tennis shoes for a massive tournament he was to play at his local tennis club.

"The night before the tournament, he left them on the shoe rack we kept at the front door, ready for the next day.

"Well, of course Bruno was quite taken with these bright white tennis shoes that he had never seen before and wanted to play with them."

"Oh no," Iris exclaimed, burying her face into the palms of her hands.

"My parents didn't allow Bruno to come upstairs at night when we were in bed, so he had all night to play with these soft, white chew toys."

Iris was laughing; her young, innocent tones filled the air with welcomed noise and hilarity. I couldn't help but smile and think to myself that she was finally free. This girl who was tortured for so long was now opening her wings and taking flight for the first time in her life. To sit and witness it was beautiful.

That was the first time in my life that I felt I had achieved something.

"When the morning came, my father came downstairs only to be greeted by shreds of white canvas from his brand-new shoes that was scattered over the floor of the hallway and into the kitchen, like the trail of breadcrumbs in Hansel and Gretel."

"What did your father do?" Iris asked excitedly, totally enthralled in the tale she was being told.

"There was nothing he could do. My father was very strict, but he was not an angry man. In fact, I don't so much as remember any time when he shouted at me or hit me. He just took Bruno by the collar, led him outside and told him he'd best not move from his kennel for the rest of the day."

"Did Bruno do as he was told?"

"Of course not, Iris! As soon as my father had left for his tennis tournament, Bruno was back out of the kennel and playing with me in the back garden."

"Bruno sounds like an amazing dog. I would love to have a dog when I'm older."

"I loved him too, Iris. He was my best friend, and,

in truth, my parents thought of him as another one of their children. We were all devastated when he died. It was like losing a member of the family."

As Dr Rosen finished telling his story, my phone rang. It was Seth telling me that he was only a few minutes away from the safehouse. He had Annyagh with him and they wanted to check how Iris was and how we were all doing.

I unlocked the door and told him to let himself in when they arrived. Iris, Dr Rosen and I sat the table finishing our drinks and waited for our guests to arrive.

Outside, it was a glorious day. The Sun was perched high in the sky and breathing life into the whole landscape around us. It presided over all it surveyed, like a gardener tending to a prize-winning garden, preening and tending to each and every imperfection that could take the shine off their achievement.

Birds soared high in the sky, playing chase games, painting patterns with their wings and making music with their calls. The smaller birds toyed with each other in the rising and falling of the breeze while their elders watched on from the trees and roof of the house, almost tutting at the actions of their offspring.

In the fields behind the house, rabbits hopped around, rising and falling like salmon through the long grass. The varying degrees of brown fur hopped up and disappeared again, as though coming up for air briefly. All of this hopping and rising and falling was done in silence, doing all they could to avoid any predators who may prey on them.

A gentle breeze made its presence known by invisibly making trees, grass and wildflowers dance a synchronised, choreographed routine for no reason other than for its entertainment and for the pleasure of onlookers like us.

Inside the house, the front door opened and closed and the sound of Annyagh's purposeful footsteps marched up the hallway and out onto the decking. Seth was a step or two behind her.

"And how are we all?" Seth asked, his tone more chipper than normal.

"Good," Iris exclaimed confidently. "Dr Rosen was just telling me a story about a pet he had when he was a little boy."

"Very good," Annyagh added. "I see Sleeping Beauty is waking from her slumber."

"Sleeping who?" asked Iris.

"Never mind, pretty girl," Annyagh said, almost apologetically. "She was a beautiful girl who was made to sleep by a wicked old lady and was woken up by a prince when he gave her true love's first kiss."

"That's disgusting!"

Everyone laughed and Annyagh flopped down beside Iris and gave her a playful hug. "I didn't mean that you were kissing boys! I was talking about your sleeping, but it's good to see you up."

"Yes, all is good," Dr Rosen added. "We seem to be coming out the other side. I have checked all of her bloods and she seems to be making great progress."

Iris smiled broadly at this. Annyagh gave her another gently squeeze.

"How is 'big sister' treating you?" asked Seth, referring to Charlotte and Erica's relationship before we left the first safehouse.

Iris looked softly at me and smiled slightly again, trying to hide it from the others. "Good."

I said nothing. I winked in acknowledgement and sipped at my drink again. I had never had a younger sister or brother but the relationship I had built up with Iris was exactly the relationship I would have imagined having.

"When will we be able to go outside?" Iris asked.

"We are outside," I replied.

"No, I mean, when can we go out *there?*" Iris gestured towards the local village.

We all knew what she meant but didn't know how to answer the question without bringing her mood down. In her mind, it probably felt like an age since we broke her out of The Institute but, in reality, it was only a few weeks and The Authorities would be scouring the country for her so taking Iris out was just not possible and would not have been possible for a long time.

How could we tell her that without shattering her?

"Soon," Annyagh answered. "Once things calm down, we will take you for some pancakes and maple syrup."

Annyagh looked over at Seth and I and shrugged her shoulders ever so slightly. She knew what she was saying was only a half truth. Yes, once things calmed down we could possibly take her out, but now long would that be? Weeks? Months? Years?

No one knew for sure but we all knew it would most likely be the latter.

Annyagh distracted Iris before she asked why by

showing her a secret handshake she claimed she used to do with the squad she was in command of in the Armed Forces.

"Okay, now turn and face me. This is a top-secret handshake that my squad and I used when we came back from a mission when I was in the Armed Forces. Now, copy me."

Annyagh went through the different stages of the handshake slowly with Iris as we all watched. I knew from Seth's facial expression that he was blown away by the progress Iris had made since the night we took her from The Institute.

Annyagh shook Iris' hand twice then bumped the front, then back, then front of their opencd hands together. She then linked little fingers with Iris, shook hands twice with Iris holding only fingertips, tapped fists top and bottom and then made fists and bumped knuckles.

"You think you've got that then?" Annyagh asked Iris, winking over towards Seth and I.

Dr Rosen just sat watching the whole scene unfold before him, smiling the whole time. I think seeing this girl blossom and open up her petals for the first time was a godsend for him. He had spent so long running tests on her, keeping her company by reading to her on nights when she was sedated and then nursing her through the torment of her treatment when weaning her off the medications she had been on for so long.

Now, this young girl was being a young girl. She was playing, conversing, exploring and experiencing the world for the first time. For Dr Rosen, the relief must have been washing over him, like a tide over a beach.

Iris worked with Annyagh to learn the handshake and made us all laugh when she mixed up parts of it and made mistakes. I had never seen her have so much fun and I had never seen Annyagh be so open and warm to anyone before.

I knew that her attitude with me at the start was all a front to see if I had what it took to stick things out at Bethlehem and with The Resistance.

Once I had proven myself, she softened towards me and saw that I had a use with my connections in the world of journalism and my connections with certain sources who had been wronged by The Authorities and Security Forces.

She was amazing with Iris.

Watching her interact with the fifteen-year-old girl in front of her made me confident to know that Iris would have someone else who would put everything on the line for her. Annyagh was a hardened military veteran but Iris had found a way to melt away that exterior Annyagh spent years trying to build up.

Finally, in the end, after ten minutes or so, Iris got the handshake and cheered with delight that she had passed this test that Annyagh had set her.

Annyagh got up to use the bathroom and get a drink while the rest of us sat and talked. Seth reached into a rucksack that he'd brought with him and lifted out a book.

"I almost forgot. I got that book you were asking me for," he said, handing a black, leather-bound book to Dr Rosen.

"Ah, yes! My favourite!"

"What is it?" asked Iris, inquisitively as usual.

"This book is special to me, Iris. When I was a young man, I would read this book to remind me of the job I was put here on Earth to do. I have read it countless times on my own and, on a few occasions, to you."

"You read it to me? I don't remember you reading a book like that with me. Anything we read together was when I was little."

"That's right, my dear, but, when you were…

asleep… I would read this to you."

Iris' mood changed slightly, instantly becoming more sombre. "I see. What is it called?"

Dr Rosen passed the book to Iris and she scanned the front cover. "*Frankenstein*, by Mary Shelley."

"One evening, you spoke to Jade about a memory you had of me reading a book to you about a creature," Dr Rosen said, pointing to the book in Iris' hands. "This is the book from your memory."

Iris sat quietly for a moment, leafing through the pages.

"What is the matter, Iris?" asked Dr Rosen, thinking he had offended her by referring to her 'sleeping'.

"I love it, thank you," Iris replied, hugging Dr Rosen.

"It's quite alright, I was just worried in case I had upset you."

"You hadn't." Iris decoupled herself from Dr Rosen. "I just feel like I have missed so much. I can't remember…"

"Don't worry about remembering, you will, soon. Jade and I will piece things together and we will help you to build a picture of what you have missed."

Iris nodded, acknowledging Dr Rosen's passionate

interruption.

"You aren't alone in this, Iris," I added, trying to help Dr Rosen reassure her.

"I know."

Dr Rosen got up to get a drink from the kitchen and left Iris, Seth and I on the decked area. Iris didn't speak and neither did Seth or I.

We felt it to be disrespectful to make small talk and have meaningless conversation with Iris when she was dealing with conflicts within herself. She also made it clear she didn't want to talk when she curled up on the chair she was sat on and began reading *Frankenstein*.

From inside the house, I heard the mumbling of voices. I got up and made my way in to see what was happening. When I got inside the door I could see Annyagh and Dr Rosen arguing. Their voices were becoming raised, so I shut the door and locked it to make sure Iris didn't get any more upset than she already was.

I turned to see Annyagh with the tablet computer in her hand and she was gesturing to it when addressing Dr Rosen. "How could you? She was just a little girl!"

"I am completely aware of how old she was and if I could go back and change…"

"We would all like to go back and change things, doctor. If I could go back and not pull the trigger on people I've killed in the past, I would, but I can't…"

"Exactly! You have done things in your past that you are ashamed of, as have I!"

"I didn't hurt children, you animal!"

"You knew what happened in The Institute before you got involved with Iris and I."

"Just stop it, now. Both of you," I interjected. Both Annyagh and Dr Rosen stopped to look at me. "He's right, Annyagh. We all knew what would have gone on inside those walls."

"And you've read this?"

"Not all of it, but a lot of it, yes. Everything Dr Rosen has told me is checking out in those records. He did do things that he regrets but we *did* know this, and we have to accept that he is on *our* side now, not the side of The Authorities and The Institute."

"They would cut her open…"

"I know," I replied.

"They drilled in through her skull and…"

"Look, Annyagh, I know. I read the exact same file before Iris came down from her room."

"That was one of my last tests that I conducted on Iris and I did it under duress. They threatened to hurt my daughter of I didn't carry out the test," Dr Rosen added.

Annyagh moved closer to Dr Rosen, almost face to face with him. "You're a monster," she whispered with venom. She held up the tablet computer. "This... all of this... you should be ashamed." Annyagh slid the tablet onto the breakfast bar and started to walk away.

"I am, my dear, tr—"

"Don't call me that! I'm not your 'dear'! I am nothing to you! No matter how hard you try to wash your hands, they will forever be stained with the actions you carried out with Iris and the others. You are an abomination and you need to tell that girl everything you and your minions did to her.

"If you don't, I will."

Annyagh walked to the door, unlocked it and, like a switch being flicked, she called to Iris, "Hey, pretty girl, we have to get back."

"Where are you going?"

"Back home."

"Yeah, we have a long journey and need to get back to organise things for something big happening tomorrow," added Seth.

Annyagh hugged Iris tightly and whispered something to her. Iris nodded in acknowledgement and Annyagh left, kissing Iris on the forehead.

As she walked through the kitchen, Annyagh glared at Dr Rosen. The look she gave him was like that I would imagine her giving one of her enemies before she shot them down where they stood and, considering how heated the argument was between them when I came in through the back doors, if she had a gun, I dare say she would have used it.

Seth came in the door a few seconds later and it was obvious to him that something had gone on or something had been said and he was not aware of the details. Rather than ask what had happened, he simply gestured with his hands upturned in front of him and shrugged his shoulders as if to ask, 'What was that all about?'

The front door closed, and I locked it after everyone had left. As I turned the key in the lock, I had no idea what I was walking back in to. Could Dr Rosen have walked out along with them and left me alone with Iris? Could he have completely shut down on us altogether? I simply didn't know.

I turned and made my way back into the kitchen and saw that Dr Rosen had not moved from the spot where I'd left him, standing with his lower back resting against the worktop and his arms folded across his chest. He had not even taken his eyes off the flashing display on the oven in front of him.

"I..."

"Don't speak, Jade," he said, his voice breaking and deeper than I'd ever heard it before, as though it was rising from the depths of a very dark pit somewhere deep inside him. "You don't have to say anything."

I didn't speak. I just listened.

"My whole life, I always convinced myself that what I did, even if it was questionable, was for the greater good – that it would help our species in the end. But now? After this?"

"She was angry, doctor."

"Yes, you're right, my dear, she was angry. I have always thought that when people are angry they tear down any barriers they may be holding up to protect others from the truth, the inconvenient truth, the truth that could be dangerous and hurtful." Dr Rosen paused and swallowed, as though trying his best to push something back down within himself. "She was right. I am a monster."

"Wilhelm…"

"Stop, Jade," he retorted, rather forcefully. It was clear that he didn't want to hear another word from me. "I need to talk to Iris. I need to come clean – not about everything, but what I feel I *can* tell her."

He walked across the kitchen and stopped at the sliding door before opening it. He turned and looked me in the eye. "Promise me you will tell her everything, Jade. Someday, when you feel the time is right, you will fill in the missing gaps I cannot."

"I promise."

Dr Rosen went out to the decking, closed the door and locked it behind him. I knew it wasn't my place to be there and listen in on a conversation between Iris and a man who was practically a father to her.

He sat down beside her and Iris closed the book. The pair of them then faced each other and Dr Rosen started to sob. Iris held his hand in both of hers and he started to talk.

Iris listened.

CHAPTER 22

That evening, everything seemed to have calmed down. Iris and Dr Rosen had their long discussion outside on the decking while I sat inside reading more of the files Dr Rosen left on the tablet computer.

The more I read of the files, the more I started to see that everything Dr Rosen was telling was the truth. There were leaked emails from Malcom Barton to other senior executives at The Institute that said Dr Rosen's daughter, Elaina, was to be used as leverage if he was to refuse to cooperate.

Everything he said was backed up in the emails.

I sat reading through files for over an hour before there was any movement indicating that Dr Rosen and Iris were going to come back inside. I sat and watched as Dr Rosen cried, then Iris comforted him.

After that, Iris would cry, and Dr Rosen would comfort her.

It was clear from watching the pair of them that there was a deep love there and Dr Rosen was truly sorry for everything that had happened to her whilst inside the walls of The Institute. It was also clear that Iris understood that he was being honest with her and that there would be no grudges or ill feeling between the pair of them.

For the last fifteen minutes or so, before the pair of them came back inside, they simply sat and hugged. Iris leant into Dr Rosen's chest and he sat with his arm around her. Neither of them moved.

They were at peace.

As an onlooker, I felt exhausted trying to gauge what was happening and what was being said between the two of them, never mind actually sitting through the whole episode in person.

When it came to dinner time, we sat round the table eating salad, cold meats and bread. We chatted about everything and anything apart from The Institute and what was discussed or had happened earlier in the day.

There was a silent, agreed consensus between the three of us that it had been dealt with and we were to move on. Whether or not Annyagh would feel the same was a different matter.

In the middle of us eating and Iris telling us her first thoughts on *Frankenstein*, the sound of a key being put into the front door came down the hallway like a sharp, serrated blade on a metallic surface. The door opened, and it was The Courier with Seth and Carl.

"We need to move, now," The Courier said sharply in his Scottish accent.

"Move? Why?" I asked, trying to hide the panic in my voice that was permeated with thuds of my heart beating in my chest.

Carl looked white as a sheet. "We've been given a tip-off from The Benefactor, The Authorities know you're in the area. They don't know exactly where you are, but they will be in the area to search soon so we need to pack and move right away."

"Iris, come with me." Dr Rosen got up with Iris and went straight upstairs to gather what few things they had.

I went to The Courier and spoke to him in the kitchen. "How bad is this? You need to tell me now."

"*You* need gather your belongings and get out before they are onto you. Do as I ask, please." The

Courier's tone cut like a blade and I left immediately to gather my things.

Within two minutes I was packed and back downstairs with everything that I owned. I lifted the tablet computer and went to put it in my bag.

"Is that the data cache from Rosen?" The Courier asked.

"Yes, I was going to…"

"Give it to me. I'll take it to The Benefactor's house. It will be safe there."

"How can I trust you?" I asked, doing my best to pin him down.

"Look, if I wanted to report you all, I would have done it already. I could have called The Authorities and the Security Forces would have you all in handcuffs and into the back of their armoured cars so fast your head would spin. This isn't about trust, this is about survival. Think about it, sweetheart, what other choice do you have?"

He was right. I couldn't do anything. I handed the tablet over and he swiftly put it into a black holdall he had on the floor beside him. "Listen, doll, when you make it to Bowmore, you can have your little piece of glass back. I don't trust the things anyway. I'm a

Courier, remember that. I don't steal – I carry items and I deliver."

"Answer my question."

"Which one?"

I turned to see if Iris and Dr Rosen had appeared from upstairs yet before I spoke. "How bad is this? Will we…?"

The Courier spoke softly to me. "I don't know. To be honest, I don't know. I can't promise you anything. All I do know is that you are to head north from here to Carlisle. There is another safehouse there. Once you are there, I will contact you and we will make arrangements for something that little bit more permanent."

I started to let the emotions bubble up within me and my eyes started to tear up. "What if we are captured? What if they take her?"

"Don't think you will be totally alone, Jade. I will be nearby. Take this." The Courier handed me a piece of paper with a phone number on it. "If something happens, anything at all and you need me, call that number. Just keep that wee lassie safe."

Just then, Dr Rosen and Iris made their way downstairs and Seth and Carl took their bags to the car. "Ready," Carl called.

"Ready," I called, trying to compose myself before turning to face Iris.

The Courier took my hand. "You can do this, you hear me? You've got her this far. Just take her a little bit further. Take her little steps at a time – baby steps."

"Baby steps," I replied, repeating his words in an attempt to calm myself.

"Now go."

I turned and made my way to Dr Rosen and Iris. "All good to go?"

"Ready," Iris replied.

"Let's go," said Dr Rosen, breathing deeper than normal, as though trying to catch his breath.

"Are you...?"

"Get into the car, Jade, we don't have time," he ordered, ushering me to the car waiting at the front door.

The five of us got into the car, Seth and Carl in the front with Dr Rosen, Iris and I in the back. Iris was sat in the middle, holding my hand tightly in hers.

"It's going to be okay, Jade," she whispered to me,

almost sensing my unease and what was unfolding before us. Pages upon pages of a blank narrative yet to be written with no clues as to how the story would end.

"I know," I replied, smiling slightly. I hated how lies tasted when I said them to Iris. They tasted like sulphur.

Carl sped off and turned down a side lane that was tree lined and more difficult for anyone to see as we left the grounds of the house. When we turned out onto the side road, leaving the place we called home for that short time behind, no cars were on the road and Carl accelerated towards the horizon.

"Where are we heading?" he asked Seth.

"North, towards Carlisle," Seth replied. "When we arrive there, we will be given more instructions."

After those words were spoken, no others left our lips for what felt like an age. The air in the car felt thick and heavy, like we could cut it with a knife. Even if words were spoken, they wouldn't have enough weight to them to be heard or survive within the confines of the car.

We passed through the local village. Shops were closing up for the night, shutters were being pulled down and the streets were clearing of shoppers and locals spending their last pounds and pennies for the day.

The buildings were all quaint and of the same type, as though the town planner used copy and paste on a computer when laying out the buildings along each street. Each sign of the shops was hand painted in the same black letters on a cream background and in the same, simple italic font.

The village was beautiful.

Passing through, I saw a little café on the corner and the waitress, no more than twenty, was carrying in the tables and chairs, closing up for the night. I couldn't take my eyes off the last few tables and chairs sitting outside. I only wished that Iris and I could have gone there and simply sat to watch the world go by. Watching the families meander from shop to shop, talking about nothing in particular while the cars trundled slowly by.

I closed my eyes as we passed the café. I could feel the Sun on my face as Iris and I sat drinking coffee and reading books. There were no Authorities or Security Forces searching for us.

In my mind, for those brief imaginary seconds, we were free.

As we drove further into the village, all of the

traffic lights stayed green, almost welcoming us to pass through junction, to junction, to junction. 'The way is clear,' the lights appeared to say.

Soon, we turned on to a main road and Carl accelerated to get us up to speed and onto the main leg of our journey north. In the silence that rang, like the deafening toll of a bell, motorbike engines could be heard from behind us.

In the rear-view mirror, I could see Carl's eyes sharpen and his brows raise. His eyes met mine and I knew the look that greeted me – fear.

As the roar of the engines drew nearer, Carl accelerated harder. From beside me, Dr Rosen's breathing quickened, and he was sweating.

"They have found us, haven't they, my dear?" Dr Rosen asked me.

I nodded in reply.

Instead of panicking, Dr Rosen's eyes wore a look of acceptance. He was a man who had confessed all of his sins earlier that afternoon. His soul was at peace and, if he were to meet his maker, so be it.

CHAPTER 23

Carl stopped the car in a layby to check on Dr Rosen, but only when he was confident he had lost the following motorbikes. Iris and I were in the back seat with him. His breathing was short, and he was gasping for breath, clutching his chest.

I can't remember much of what was said from Carl or Seth in the front of the car. Everything was moving in slow motion and their voices were so distant I could barely make out a word they said as Seth and Carl opened their doors and scrambled to Dr Rosen's door to help him.

They lifted him out and lay him at the roadside. Seth was calling someone from The Resistance frantically, trying to do what he could to get hold of someone who could tell him what to do. The Resistance did have doctors who were always on call to assist, but none of them would have been able to get to us – to Dr Rosen.

We got out and stood at the roadside, looking down on this man struggling to breathe and who was slipping away before our eyes. In all the chaos, Iris remained still. She stood over Dr Rosen and barely moved. Instead, she stood there, staring at him, analysing him, as though searching for something intangible.

In what seemed like slow motion, Iris knelt down beside Dr Rosen and took his hand in hers, never taking her eyes off his. It was as though there was a telepathic connection between the pair of them, something no one else could see, feel or touch – an intimate pathway between two souls that were intrinsically linked through circumstances and an apparent necessity to save lives.

Dr Rosen's breathing settled, and he smiled. A single tear rolled down his cheek and into the dirt on the roadside. Everything around us was calm. Seth stopped frantically dialling his phone, Carl stopped pulling at Dr Rosen's shirt to put on the defibrillator and I stood motionless, watching the exchange between doctor and patient – between 'father' and 'daughter'.

Iris cupped her second hand round Dr Rosen's and brought his hand to her lips, kissing it gently, as though releasing him from the burden he had carried with him daily.

With the kiss that laid and left his hand, like the landing of a butterfly on the head of a summer flower, Dr Rosen exhaled one final time and his arm fell limp onto Iris' lap.

No one moved.

For that short amount of time, no one knew what to say, how to react or what to do. Iris was the only one who reacted. She squeezed his hand and laid it by his side. Iris then knelt over his face, kissed his forehead and used the tips of the fingers on her left hand to close his eyes. Dr Rosen was finally at peace.

Iris stood up and spoke four words. "We need to leave."

The four of us slowly and hesitantly made our way to the car, closed the doors and Carl sped off. I turned to look back at the roadside. After the dust had settled, I could see the body of a man appear through the clearing cloud. For many years, he was part of the system that we were trying to tear down, brick by brick, but in the time I had known him, he had done all that he could to redeem himself – he had paid his penance.

"What do we do now?" Carl asked, in his usual panicking tone.

"We keep going," replied Seth. "Everything we have worked for will be for nothing if we don't make it to the safehouse. Just keep driving. I'll contact Annyagh to find out where she is." Seth started dialling the numbers on his phone, but we were out in the middle of the countryside and the phone couldn't get a signal.

Seth's frustration would be made audible with the odd, 'Come on,' and, 'We need to get a signal, Carl.' To which Carl would respond with an argumentative statement instead of trying to help the situation.

Iris and I sat in the back of the car holding hands. She hadn't taken her eyes off the back of Seth's seat since we got into the car. I knew that inside her head she was processing all that had happened to her in the past twenty-four hours.

Her mood would surely have gone from high, to low, to high again like a rollercoaster through the course of the day. Iris would even have got some answers from Dr Rosen out on the decked area before dinner and The Courier came to tell us we had to leave.

I looked at her face and started to wonder if things would ever level out for her, if she would ever have anything resembling a normal life... if I could keep her safe and alive long enough to experience life.

The engine of the car sang, changing tones with every gear change. Carl tried not to speed so as to not attract the attention of The Authorities.

Every time we stopped at a set of traffic lights, Seth and Carl scanned all around them, looking through every window, to check if there was any sign of the two motorcycles that had started to give chase not long after we left The Benefactor's safehouse.

I sat holding Iris' hand the whole time and tried not to think about the Security Forces' motorcycles or how we were going to get to the next safehouse. All I was concerned about was how Iris was feeling and what she was thinking about since we left Dr Rosen by the side of the road.

"We'll be okay, you know," Iris said quietly.

"I know," I replied, reassuringly, even if I didn't fully believe it myself.

"We are being followed and we are being watched, but it will all be okay," she turned and looked me in the eye, her irises glistening in the light, like the chatoyance of a gemstone. "I believe that everything we have done has been for a purpose and that purpose hasn't happened yet."

I smiled and held Iris' hand that little bit tighter, feeling comfort in the words this teenage girl was saying to me. Her words were an antidote to the panic and chaos that was enveloping us.

Carl drove off at the green light of a junction and the glass of the window beside him popped loudly, shattering into thousands of pieces, like confetti, showering us all in fragments of glass, like imperfect diamonds.

Carl clutched his shoulder and lurched to the side as he accelerated.

Seth grappled with the wheel. "Drive! Just drive!"

"I've been hit! It's my shoulder!"

I looked out the window, towards where the shot had come from and saw one of the men in black and red leather climb back onto his motorbike, while speaking into a radio.

I turned to look at Iris and her expression had not changed. It was as though she saw two moves ahead and could picture our fates, like the screen of a cinema, she could watch the scenes unravel before her eyes.

Carl turned right into an industrial area and told us to get out. We jumped out of the car and, before we could speak, Carl sped off back out of the gate and away from the warehouses.

Seth grabbed us, and we dove in behind a selection of barrels. Off to our left, we heard the roar of a motorbike engine and a second or two later the two black bikes sped off up the road after the car and Carl as we held our breath, hoping they would not turn around and figure out where we were.

"What about Carl?" I asked Seth.

"He'll be fine. He knows what he's doing."

"But what if they catch him? They'll…"

"We all know the dangers this mission brought with it," Seth whispered in a venomous tone. "The priority is Iris, we need to keep her safe." Seth nudged us towards the open door of a warehouse. "Over there! Go!"

We crouched down and ran across to the opened door, closing it behind us. The metallic slam of the latch catching in the lock sounded too similar to the closing of the doors in The Institute. I couldn't help but think about how, if we were caught, Iris would have gone full circle – from cell, to a captive freedom, to a cell awaiting capture.

Iris looked at me and took my hand. "It will be okay. Carl will be okay."

CHAPTER 24

The evening passed slowly. We sat silently behind a stack of barrels in the corner of the warehouse for what seemed like an eternity. The workers in the warehouse, like termites, scuttled around, loading barrels on and off lorries and vans.

I thought over and over again about what might happen if we were spotted by one of the termites. What would they say? Would they help us by pretending they'd never laid eyes on us or would they report us to The Authorities?

Fortunately, none of this happened and we were able to sit in our sanctuary undisturbed until the warehouse door slammed shut for the night. The sound of the metal door slamming solidly into the metal frame sent a loud, metallic thud echoing around the empty, dull warehouse. The sound rolled around the walls, gradually dissipating and losing energy until it was nothing but a whisper and then fell to silence.

Seth stayed down and peeked out to check that everyone had gone. Once he was happy, he made his way across to the access panel on the wall beside the door and set his phone against it. Carl developed an app that could be used to strip the access code from the panel into his phone's memory. This was one thing I loved about Carl, his creativity and ingenuity. When Carl saw a problem, he did his absolute best to find a solution and, with his tech mind, he was normally able to code a program that could be used by The Resistance in many different ways.

"Who needs a key?" Seth said, turning and smiling at us as we made our way from behind the barrels.

The emergency lighting lit the warehouse just enough for us to feel secure in a strange place. The dull, orange glow cast enough light from the lights dotted around the ceiling to make colours we once knew into more exotic, foreign colours we'd rarely if ever seen before.

Along all of the walls were stacks of barrels of varying heights, like termite mounds. In the dull light, we could barely see the colours of the barrels – some red, some blue and some black – against a backdrop of dull yellow metal walls.

The Authorities made it illegal to waste power when businesses were supposed to be closed and it was law to have reduced 'security lighting' or to have the lights off completely. We were just happy to have ran into a warehouse that chose the security lighting. The thought of being locked inside a pitch-black warehouse all night with the Security Forces hunting us down would probably have sent us all over the edge.

Seth paced around, trying to find a signal to call Annyagh to let her know we hadn't made it to the safehouse. I liked to think he was totally calm, our great leader, but I also took some comfort in the fact that he was pacing around. This glimpse of anxiety shown by Seth was new to me but, if he wasn't anxious at all, part of me thought I would be more concerned.

Anxiety made him look human – more like us.

I sat against a stack of barrels with Iris laying on an old dustsheet beside me, her head resting on my lap. "It's so quiet in here."

"I know," I replied, "all of the warehouses have closed for the night."

"Will anyone come for us?"

"Yes, it won't be long."

"Is that why Seth is walking round so much?" Iris asked, watching the man walk around with his phone out in front of him saying words he wouldn't want Iris to hear under his breath.

"Yes, he's trying to get help for us." I sat stroking Iris' hair and Seth looked over with an exasperated expression on his face before turning and climbing the stack of barrels behind him towards a window where he could get a signal from the outside.

I knew why he didn't want to go out the main door. The fact that the main lights would come on, attracting attention from any passing Security Forces, was too much of a risk for us to take. At least if he was able to get a signal from within the warehouse, the main light sensors wouldn't think someone was entering the building and light up the whole inside.

As Seth perched himself on top of the Christmas tree of dull red barrels I could barely see him give us a thumbs-up that he'd got a signal. After a few seconds, I heard his side of the conversation with Annyagh.

Hey, it's me.

No, we were ambushed.

Only Iris, Jade and myself. Carl was shot in the shoulder and drove off to lure them away.

245

Two on bikes.

I don't know, I haven't heard from him. Have you?

No? I just hope he got away.

Yeah, me too. Are you at the safehouse?

Okay, well use my signal to get our location. We're in a large, yellow warehouse. The compound is well lit so you should be able to see it okay. Opposite us is a red McAllister Freight warehouse with two lorries parked outside it.

Good. Get here as quick as you can. I'll lower down a sheet for you to climb up. We don't want to use the door, at least until morning.

How long do you think you'll be?

Good. See you then.

Seth scrambled back down the barrels and made his way over to us. "She's at the safehouse and is leaving now. It won't be long, Iris. We'll get you to safety, don't worry."

Iris sat up and smiled in acknowledgement of what Seth said. She then looked up to me, casting me a look of worry for the first time. She didn't know Seth. To her, he was a face and a name. There was no depth to him, no trust that had been built up between them, like she had done with myself, Dr Rosen and, even to some extent, Annyagh.

I trusted Seth but that didn't matter. I don't think the lack of trust between Iris and Seth was the problem. Iris had a feeling that something wasn't right and, for the first time in a long time, I was scared.

CHAPTER 25

Later that evening, Seth got a call from Annyagh to say that she had arrived at the compound. She was parked across the road in a fast food restaurant car park and was talking to Seth as she waited to check if she had been followed.

Seth scaled the mountain of barrels again, bringing the conjoined dust sheets that we had tied together to make one long 'rope' for Annyagh to climb up.

Are you sure you weren't followed?

Definitely?

How long have you been in the car for?

Give it another five minutes just to make sure.

Seth took a torch out of his pocket and flashed it across at Annyagh in the car park across the road.

Can you see me?

Good. When the five minutes is up, come over and I'll lower the sheet down for you to climb up.

No, still no word from him.

I know, I know, but remember Iris is the priority. We've come too far to turn back now.

I knew he was talking about Carl and from the one side of the conversation I'd heard, I knew that Annyagh hadn't heard from him either.

Inside, I felt a pang of something. I was unsure whether it was love, guilt, worry or grief. I knew I didn't love Carl, but I also knew I cared for him a great deal and would never have wanted anything bad to happen to him. He was someone I considered a close friend and, whether or not we were to patch things back up again after Iris was safe, I wanted him to have given the Security Forces the slip – I wanted Carl to be safe.

But I also knew that chances of that were slim.

Okay, if you're sure. Make your way over towards the window that I'm flashing the torch from and I'll drop the sheets.

Seth hung up the phone and I scaled the barrels to help him hoist Annyagh in.

Iris was sitting on the floor, leaning against a crate, reading one of the books she'd managed to bring with her when leaving the house. She was calm looking on the outside but the jiggling of her feet as she was reading made me feel she was starting to feel uneasy as the night wore on.

When I reached the top of the barrels, I tied the end of the sheets to one of the roof supports above our heads and Seth lowered the sheets down to Annyagh, who had just scaled a fence and was making her way across the compound with a large hold-all over her shoulder.

"Take this first," she whispered while tying the handles of the large bag onto the bottom of the sheet. Seth and I hoisted it up to the window.

There was a lot of weight in the bag and it took both of us to angle it through the window. Seth held on to the sheet while I pulled the hold-all in and set it on the next layer of barrels just below our feet. The bag was zipped closed, but I knew what was in it. Annyagh was an expert with weapons and I was in no doubt that she had come prepared for every eventuality, even if it involved having to defend ourselves or even clear a path out of the compound.

Annyagh pulled herself up the sheet without what looked like the slightest bit of trouble or effort. I offered her a hand when she reached the window and she took hold of it in a vice-like grip and hopped in through the opened window.

I felt that she only took my hand out of politeness and I only offered it to look like I was making myself useful. I wasn't one of those tech-minded people, tactical people or a leader of men. My job was to look after a fifteen-year-old girl and I tried to take some comfort in that fact as those around me appeared to take on more forward, active roles in other aspects of the mission.

The whole time I knew Annyagh, I rarely had more than the slightest of conversations with her and, when I first arrived at The Resistance with Carl, I thought she hated me.

During meetings and discussion sessions, she would almost sneer at any points or answers I offered up and would usually come up with a point to oppose mine, just to make me look small in front of the others.

Carl always told me not to worry about it, but it was hard when the little jibes were so regular and so consistently negative.

Through the time I got to know her, I saw that there was more to the person who appeared to go out of her way to make me feel unwelcome. Once I showed that I was there to stay and offer up information on stories that sources had shared with me, Annyagh softened slightly towards me.

That and the fact that more new faces were showing up with the hope of joining The Resistance and she redirected her focus and negative comments towards them.

She was older than me, thirty-five years old, and had a military background but was discharged when her views on certain conflicts The Authorities were leading the Armed Forces into differed from that of her superiors. Annyagh told me one evening, when we were planning some of the points for a lesser, disruptive mission to knock out the power to a Security Forces base, that she spent so much of her time towards the end of her career in the Armed Forces arguing with orders she was given from her superiors.

"I couldn't agree with them," she said. "At the start, I carried out the orders like some robot and didn't think about it. Then I remember one night when I woke up having night terrors. I remember opening my eyes to see one of the villagers I killed pinning me down on the bed, shouting at me in his own language. I was petrified and was paralysed with fear.

"I couldn't understand what he was saying apart

from one word, 'Muuaji! Muuaji!' It was what some of the villagers would call us as we moved to place to place.

"It meant 'murderer'.

"That night, was the start of it. My priorities started to change, and I began questioning orders. I refused to let my squad carry out orders that I knew were wrong.

"I was then taken off active duty, thrown in a cell and, in the end, dishonourably discharged."

I looked up to Annyagh. She was a strong person, both inside and out. Her body was solid and toned and her skin was decorated with tattoos – some from her days in the Armed Forces and others to commemorate times in her life. The most striking tattoo was that of an eye on her chest. It was to recognise her refusal to just accept what she was told by her superiors and to finally open her eyes to see what The Authorities, Armed and Security Forces were doing to people.

Her short, manly haircut made her look tough and she was so very physically strong. So many nights, I would see her in the exercise room in Bethlehem, 'relieving herself of stress' as she would say, lifting weights and punching or kicking a heavy bag. As I would watch her move around the bag, punching, kicking and slashing at it with a practice knife, I would liken her movements to a ballerina. Annyagh would move gracefully, lightly on her feet but strike with sickening, deadly blows that would send the heavy punch bag swinging away from her.

At times, I felt there was a tension between her and Seth. Sometimes, Annyagh could be heard shouting and arguing with him about how he was being too rash and putting people in danger with his pursuit of 'petty missions' as she would say. She would also argue with him about how he was wasting resources or not doing enough when, in her opinion, the time was right to strike a Security Forces patrol or kidnap an official to get intelligence that could help locate people of interest to The Resistance.

It was clear that she was hot headed and, if she were in charge of The Resistance, things would have been a lot different and most probably reckless at times. Seth saw the bigger picture better than Annyagh did, but Annyagh understood the tactical side and had the military background to call upon when it was needed – and we needed her.

As Annyagh stood up after climbing in through the window, she nodded at me before hopping down to scoop up her bag and making her way onto the floor of the warehouse.

"Hey there, pretty girl," she called out to Iris. "What are you reading?"

"*Alice in Wonderland*," she replied. "I promised Dr Rosen that I would finish it."

There was a moment of silence between us all, not knowing what to say next.

Iris began to read aloud, "Now, here, you see, it takes all the running you can do, to keep in the same place. If you want to get somewhere else, you must run at least twice as fast as that." She paused for a second and looked up to address us. "All we seem to do is run. We leave The Institute, we run. We leave the first safehouse, we run. We leave the second safehouse, we run." Iris paused for a beat. "Where are we going to run to next?"

"We have a plan, Iris," interrupted Seth. "Things will work out as we planned. You'll see."

Iris looked at me to see if I would react, but I didn't. Instead of adding anything to what Seth said, she gave me a knowing look and went back to reading *Alice in Wonderland*.

Annyagh unzipped the large black bag and started

lifting out the weapons she'd brought with her. She had three machine guns and three pistols with lots of magazines of ammunition for both.

Annyagh handed a pistol to Seth and he walked off, tucking it into the back of his trousers. She then slapped a magazine into another pistol and handed it to me. I took it and she leant in to speak to me before letting it go. "This could go south, fast. I know you don't like these things but you're better to have it than not."

"Do you think we'll get out of here?" I asked, almost not wanting to know her answer.

"We have to wait until morning and get to the car I've left across the road. They are looking for us and they haven't found Carl yet. We just need to make it through the night and see what tomorrow brings."

Annyagh walked off, tucking the pistol into the back of her trousers, and sat down beside Iris. "Do you mind if I read with you?"

"No, that's fine," Iris replied, opening the book more so that Annyagh could see it.

"I haven't read this book since I was a little girl."

"Really? I like it. The world Lewis Carroll describes in it is so magical."

"I know what you mean, beautiful." Annyagh looked up at me and looked right into my eyes. "Things just keep getting curiouser and curiouser."

CHAPTER 26

"Get up, Jade. Get up quick," whispered Annyagh sharply as she shook me awake. "They're here."

I sat up and stood up so fast I felt dizzy. "How? Did you not see them?"

"They've just started to arrive in the car park across the road. I think they're checking out the car I used to get here."

Annyagh and I rushed up the stack of barrels to see what was happening outside. We could hear the hum of engines arriving. Some were smaller, like motorbikes and others were larger, like armoured cars and vans. The noises brought about an impending doom inside me. I looked out and felt like a young timid animal being surrounded and preyed upon by a pack of wild dogs.

As Annyagh and I peered out of the window, we

were taken aback by the sight that greeted us. My heart began to race inside my chest and my breathing started to quicken.

Annyagh looked across at me, wide eyed, but not in a way that looked like she was afraid. If anything, the look she gave me was one of focus and determination. She knew what was going to happen and she knew what had to be done. Inside Annyagh, it was like a switch was flicked, changing her mindset to one she would have been trained to use in combat.

I wouldn't say that the look Annyagh gave me calmed me, but it felt safer having her there with us – with Iris.

I'd never seen anything like it. The whole compound was surrounded. Everywhere we looked, there were Security Forces, all dressed in black and red. Some of them were wearing lighter body armour but others were wearing the heavier Mech Suits. These suits were made for what The Authorities wanted the Security Forces to do – storm the building.

The Security Forces must have followed Annyagh somehow. She did wait for a long time in the car park across the street, but it wouldn't have mattered if she stayed there for twice that length of time. She was right, they weren't following her in person. There must have been a tracking device on the car she had used to get her from the safehouse to where we were hiding.

The Security Forces let Annyagh lead them right to us.

Seth spoke sharply from behind us as he climbed the barrels. "This is all your fault, Annyagh!"

This was the first time I had ever seen Annyagh even slightly flustered. "I wasn't followed, I swear! I looped back on myself a million times and stopped to wait and let cars pass me if I thought I was being tailed. Trust me…"

"I did, Annyagh," Seth snapped, obviously feeling the strain of the situation he found himself in. Now he wasn't just a minder for Iris – he was her guardian and protector. "There must have been something! Someone must have followed you! You must have…"

"I wasn't," Annyagh hissed, her forehead almost touching Seth's. She was like a coiled snake, ready to pounce. Annyagh then looked over to Iris and I. "We need to hide Iris." Annyagh got up. "This way, come on."

Iris and I followed Annyagh across the warehouse where she started knocking on barrels with her knuckles. "What are you doing?" I asked.

"Find an empty barrel. We punch some airholes in it and then close it up."

"They'll find her."

"It's the only option we have. All we can hope is that she makes it out of here."

"And what about you?" Iris asked in a worried tone, seeing now that her reassuring words about everything being fine were soon to be proven wrong.

"Help me, Jade," replied Annyagh, knowing full well that the answer to the question she was asked would not be a wise one to share.

Iris tugged on my arm as I went to help Annyagh search. "Please, Jade, I want to go with you. Can we please just go?"

I turned and knelt down in front of Iris, looking her right in the eye and seeing my reflection as I did so. "It'll be okay," I lied. "We just need to put you inside one of these barrels in case they take us away." I was unconvincing. I wouldn't have believed myself if I were Iris, and even *I* didn't believe a word of what I said.

"If they take you away, will you come back to find me?"

I paused. I saw myself in her mirror-like irises. "I will."

I hugged Iris just as Annyagh called from behind the stack of barrels in front of us, "I've got one, quick!"

I ran around with Iris and we moved the barrel to the front; Annyagh already had the lid off and was checking there was nothing in it. "It smells awful, but it'll do the job."

Annyagh then took her combat knife and hammered it in to the side of the barrel about ten times to make some air holes. By the time she was done, they were large enough that I could have pushed my finger into them.

"Quick Iris, get in," I said as I lifted her up and set her into the barrel. When I set her down and tried to let her go, she clung to me, both arms wrapped tightly around my neck.

"I love you, Jade," she said, almost crying. Her voice was shaking with emotion. The tone of her voice was shaking me to my very core. My heart was breaking.

I held her tightly, feeling the warmth of her breath against my neck for what I knew would probably be the last time. "It'll be okay. Just stay in here and don't make a sound. I'll be right back, I promise." As the word 'promise' left my mouth I felt sick to the very pit of my stomach. I wouldn't be back. I wouldn't see things through to the end. I wouldn't be able to protect her like I promised her I would. Instead, I was yet another dishonest liar in a chain of lousy adults that had blown in and out of her life.

I kissed Iris on the cheek and pressed down on her shoulders to make her crouch down. Iris sat down in the huge barrel and I set the lid on top.

Annyagh and I then set another empty barrel on top of Iris' to make it look like it was part of the stack that had been already arranged. As we walked off, away from Iris, I whispered to Annyagh, "What if no one comes for her? What if…"

"Someone *will* come. Even if she is taken out of here by a delivery driver, it's better than what they'll do to her once they get their hands on her." Annyagh's eyes had turned cold, unfeeling and emotionless. She had no idea whether someone would come or if we or Iris would be safe. "Here," she said as she handed me her machine gun.

I took it and held it with both of my hands clasped tightly around it. One hand on the grip and the other on the hand guard below the barrel.

I hadn't used a gun in a while. I expected it to feel cold and detached from me – like it was alien, but it didn't. Annyagh's hands had warmed up the metal and the gun felt welcome to my touch.

I knew what was going to happen, but I also knew that I promised to protect Iris and, with a gun in my hands, I knew I would be able to do more than without it.

Annyagh paced off hurriedly towards Seth and I took out the phone from my pocket and started to compose a message.

To: Benefactor

Sorry to message like this. No safehouse. Surrounded by SF. Send help. J.

I sent the message and lifted the lid off the empty barrel above Iris' and dropped the phone inside. I was never the kind of person to just accept fate without taking one last chance, rolling the dice one last time, just in case my luck hadn't ran out just yet.

"They're coming in through the gate," Seth called from the window above us. "They're onto us. This is it."

Seth got up and clambered down the barrels and onto the ground, as he walked towards us, I noticed his left hand shaking just before he slapped it onto the handguard on the barrel of the gun.

He saw that I had noticed his hand trembling but said nothing.

"We thought this might happen," Annyagh said, firmly. "When we planned this mission, we knew things could go this way and all we can do is make a stand and hope that Iris gets out of this alive.

"When we open this door, I'll take point and cover us. Seth, you get to cover as soon as possible. Jade, you stay behind the steel door and take shots when you can. Your priority is Iris. They won't want to hurt her.

"Are we good?" asked Annyagh, drawing on the years of experience she had to remain calm and in control of whatever chaos was about to ensue.

Seth and I nodded. Seth a little less vigorously than I. Annyagh turned her back and made her way to the door, checking her weapon as she did. She then double checked where her spare magazines were in case she needed them quickly.

Annyagh turned to me and gave me a nod. 'This is it,' the nod said.

I replied by nodding back. 'I know.'

Seth scanned his phone against the access panel and Annyagh burst out the door and ran to cover behind a group of barrels just outside the door.

Seth stood still.

"Seth! Come on!" Annyagh yelled as she was coming under fire.

Seth stood still.

"Seth!" I shouted into his face, but he was petrified. He was shaking and couldn't do so much as lift his gun.

I looked out at Annyagh, pinned down behind the barrels as they were pelted with round after round of bullets. I knew I had to do something, so I ran out to take the position I knew she had told Seth to get to as soon as she had found cover.

"What are you doing, Jade? You're supposed to be protecting Iris!"

"I am! I can't just stand there and leave you stuck here. Iris won't stand a chance if we don't try something!"

Annyagh, nodded at me before turning towards Seth and calling him something, a name, I couldn't hear with all of the gunfire.

The Security Forces were moving into position to surround us. The compound was already swarming with men in red and black uniforms with body armour and weapons. They moved up every time behind men with shields – tall, clear barriers that would protect them from much of what we had to throw at them.

The closer they got to us, I knew right away that there was no escape. I just hoped that Iris would get out and get to safety. I hoped that The Benefactor would be watching over us, like some kind of guardian angel, and save her.

I had a group of them in my sights and fired. I tried not to think about what it was that I was doing. I never wanted to take lives or to hurt anyone, but I made a promise to Iris and I wanted to make sure I didn't break it.

As the group I fired at pulled back, trailing a wounded officer with them, the barrels I was crouching behind were peppered with bullets. The metallic sound of the bullets ricocheting off the barrels behind me rang out sharply, doing what they could to fight against the thundering gunshots and the screams of Seth, Annyagh and the men gradually surrounding us.

I watched as they moved in closer still. Everything around me started to slow and I was powerless to do anything.

I was a passenger.

I saw Annyagh crouched down behind a few barrels. She was mouthing words to me, doing her best to hold them off while firing around the side of the barrels.

The shooting stopped briefly, and she went to move to another group of barrels but was hit. Annyagh sprinted off out of sight behind me and I heard the gunfire start up again.

I'll never forget the noise she made as she was shot. She screamed aloud and then the gunfire stopped again.

I was terrified.

I set my gun on the ground and took out some of the off-white dust sheet that I had in my pocket. The gunfire hadn't started up again. I looked across at Seth, who was crouched down just inside the door of the warehouse.

There was fear in his eyes. I could see it. *Coward*, I thought to myself. He was someone who claimed to be brave and be everything to The Resistance, but he hid and let Annyagh and I defend Iris.

Seth was shaking as he crouched down watching me clutch the rag of sheet in my hand. Slowly, he shook his head, knowing exactly what I was thinking.

I raised my hands in the air and waved the rag.

No one shot.

Gradually, I stood up and stepped out from behind the barrels.

I was exposed.

"Where is she?" one of the Security Forces called, his helmet and mask distorting his voice. Not too dissimilar from The Benefactor's voice on the phone.

"Iris isn't here."

"We aren't going to ask again!"

"A car collected her in the middle of the night," I lied again, trying my best to stall and buy us even a few more precious seconds. I knew they probably wouldn't believe me, but I had to try.

"We know she is in there with you. One last chance, where is she? Send her out to us and you can survive this."

I breathed in slowly and closed my eyes as I exhaled. Above me, a bird called and swooped high to low in the sky. Up in the hills, the glint of something shiny caught my eye, like it was calling the bird to rest on the branches of a tree to watch what was about to unfold before it.

My heart rate didn't rise, it didn't fall, it stayed

constant, beating soundly in my chest. The blood within me coursed through my arteries and veins, from organ to muscle, to tissue and to cell.

Iris was part of me, she was blood. I had protected her as long as I could. I didn't break my promise knowingly, instead the promise was broken for me.

As I opened my eyes, a tear ran down my cheek. Like the gentle hand of a spirit stroking my face, calming me, telling me everything would be ok – it soothed my soul.

"Iris is safe! Away from here and away from you." My words rolled around the compound, echoing as the sound waves bounced from wall to wall and up into the sky above. "Iris is free!"

The gunfire started, and I fell back.

I wasn't in pain. I didn't feel anything. I just exhaled, and I rose up as my body fell to the ground.

I saw Seth run out of the warehouse, firing off in all directions.

From a distance, one shot was fired, and Seth went down holding his thigh. The officers closest to him rushed up behind their shield and kicked away his gun.

It was then that they handcuffed him and dragged him away.

As he passed my body, lying on the ground, he called to me. "I'm sorry!" he screamed. "This is all my fault! I'm so sorry, Jade."

I tried to answer.

I tried to reply but my voice was weightless and drifted away into the ether. It rose higher and higher into the sky and blew away with the wind, like dried autumn leaves in an updraft.

CHAPTER 27

I watched as the Security Forces trailed the bodies over in a row in front of the entrance of the warehouse. There were eight officers in red and black uniforms, Annyagh and then myself.

I looked peaceful, like I'd just fallen asleep where they had laid me. It was as though those who shot me took great care not to make me look a mess. My mother would have said I was pretty if she saw me. She never was one to compliment me but, seeing myself look so peaceful and pale, I knew my mother would approve.

Seth was still alive and was screaming in a mixture of pain and insults at the Security Forces for shooting me, "She was unarmed!" he screamed over and over again as he looked at my body lying on the ground beside him.

I watched Seth and couldn't help but think that this was the real Seth – the one that he'd kept from the rest of The Resistance all along.

Carl had always said that he was a fake and, as I watched him, I felt bad because he was right all along. Between Seth hiding as Annyagh and I shot at the Security Forces, seeing him shake in the doorway and then watching him cry uncontrollably, I knew he was a broken man.

The real Seth was there for everyone to see.

It wasn't long before I heard one of the Security Forces come out of the warehouse saying that Iris was unaccounted for. I was so relieved to hear that they hadn't found her.

As the events unfolded before me, I felt it was just a matter of time before Iris was carried out of the warehouse and brought back to The Institute – back to the life we'd taken her from.

If you can even call it a life.

"What do you mean she's not there? She has to be," shouted the commanding officer, insulted at the incompetence his subordinate was showing. "If you want to have a career that lasts beyond today, get back in there and tear that place apart!"

"Yes…" Before the young officer could finish his reply, his body was flung backwards from a silent gunshot that left him lifeless in an instant.

"Get down! Get to cover, now," the commanding officer screamed, sprinting to the cover of the armoured car he'd just got out of. As he dove in behind it, another silent bullet bounced off the bulletproof glass.

The Security Forces all scattered to dive behind barrels, crates and armoured cars – anything that would give them protection from what appeared to be a sharpshooter who could not be placed.

The sharpshooter was like an Angel of Death, blowing sharply onto people to simply take their lives and their souls to wherever he came from. This terrifying breath of execution caused chaos in the compound and the Security Forces could only pray that they escaped with their lives.

All around, bodies fell as panic ensued. "It's coming from the trees up on the hill," one officer called aloud before he was struck down, his words silenced before they could be elaborated on.

The officers managed to compose themselves and use the large, clear shields to help get those still living into the armoured cars and circle the bodies on the ground. The bullets that rained down on them from the hill bounced off the cars as the Security Forces lifted the bodies of their fellow officers off the ground and into the backs of the armoured cars. They also took mine and Annyagh's bodies, slammed the heavy doors shut and sped out of the compound.

Four of the Security Forces screamed up the hill beside the warehouse on motorbikes to search for a gunman while the rest drove off with Seth in handcuffs but, thankfully, no Iris.

All around the deserted compound, hopes and dreams lay in tatters.

The hopes of the Security Forces, who entered the compound and warehouse to bring Iris back to The Institute were scattered all around the bodies of their fallen colleagues. The girl they came to save and return to her 'rightful place' was still safe inside the warehouse.

The dreams of The Resistance, of Annyagh and of myself were reduced to ashes. We had lost everything protecting Iris from The Authorities and Security Forces, but I didn't regret one minute of the time I had spent with her.

Iris had not only saved millions of people from diseases and illness, she had saved me and given me a purpose. I had grown to love her like a sister and ultimately gave my life to protect her and deep down inside, whatever it was that I had become, I knew she was safe and was probably scared knowing I wasn't going to be coming back like I had promised her.

Inside the warehouse, inside the barrel, Iris sobbed. For the first time in her life, she was totally alone.

Before, when she was in The Institute, she had all of the doctors and nurses, as well as Dr Rosen, to look after her every need. Anything her body needed to survive, it was given. She may have simply been existing and not living, but unless something terrible happened during one of her tests or procedures, there was little chance of her being allowed to fall ill or die.

After we broke her out, she had Dr Rosen again to look after her medicines and help her regain her life. She also had me to do everything for her as well as be there for her when she needed someone to love her, comfort her and to confide in.

At that point, in that barrel, Iris felt more alone than she'd ever felt in her life. At times, she would peer through the air holes in the side of the barrel to see if someone was coming to save her.

No one came.

Sometimes, she called out quietly for help. Her voice was dry and raspy and barely made it out of the holes in the barrel. Again, she hoped that someone would hear and that someone would come to help her.

No one came.

She sipped on the water that Annyagh had set into the barrel, not knowing how long it would be until someone, anyone, came to her aid.

After a few hours, one armoured car returned and sat outside the warehouse. No more gunshots were fired from the hill, so they felt safe enough to get out of the car and search the warehouse one last time.

After they came out and checked if anyone had been or gone with the security guard on the gate, the officers left, appearing to believe the last words I said, that Iris was free and that she had indeed left the warehouse the night before.

The heat in the barrel was rising. She had got used to the smell, but it was starting to give her a sore head. Iris tried to sleep. With her legs held into her chest, almost hugging them as she would have done with me when she was scared, she drifted in and out of sleep.

It wasn't that she was relaxed or comfortable enough to sleep. Instead, it was exhaustion from the events of the past twenty-four hours that made her eyelids leaden and her mind drift into slumber.

As the Sun began to set in the sky, a van pulled up to the front gate and the security guard checked the ID of the driver. The driver of the van sat patiently, waiting for the security guard to raise the barrier and let him drive in.

Soon enough, the security guard checked his logs and the barrier rose. The driver was waved in through the gate and pulled up in front of the warehouse, just where I fell when the bullets hit me.

The driver backed the van up to the shutter doors and hopped out of the cabin. He made his way over to the access panel and held his white card against it. The lock on the door popped open and the lights flickered on inside and all around the warehouse.

I saw why Seth didn't want us using any doors when Annyagh arrived the night before. The lights coming on would have been like a flame for moths to be drawn to.

Inside, the driver took off his gloves and put his notes away in his jacket pocket. He took out his torch and then a hand gun from the back of his trousers.

Every time he passed a stack of crates or barrels he searched behind them carefully. As he moved, there wasn't a sound. Unlike the Security Forces, who rarely did anything quietly, this driver moved like a shadow from corner to corner and from barrel to crate. Once he was happy that he was the only person in the warehouse, a gentle knocking sound came from a far corner, causing the driver to spin around swiftly and point his gun towards the area the noise was coming from.

Iris called from inside the barrel, again, her voice too weak to penetrate the walls of the steel cylinder. Using her balled fist, she hit the side of the barrel, not caring who this person was. All Iris knew was that he was there, and he could get her out. She was unable to see the gun pointed at the barrel she was in. The airholes were too small to see in much detail.

The driver found the barrel from which the knocking noise was coming. He ran his hand over the side before knocking on it himself with his gun. The bright, metallic sound told the driver one thing. "It's empty," he said to himself quietly in his Scottish accent.

The driver then noticed the airholes pierced through the side of the barrel. They were punched out in the shape of a capital 'A'. *Annabelle*, the driver said to himself, his heart pounding like a hammer in his chest.

He put his ear to the side of the barrel and could hear sobbing and sniffling. "Iris?"

The sniffling stopped sharply.

"Iris, I'm a friend of Jade's. I drove you to the safehouses. I'm here to help you." The driver took off his hat and rubbed the top of his head.

His sense of relief was palpable, as was mine. I realised now that The Benefactor had got The Courier to come to the warehouse. The Benefactor really was Iris' guardian and The Courier was her protector.

I just hoped he could protect her better than I could.

After a few seconds, there was a reply. Her voice was frail and timid, like she'd seen something that had frightened the life out of her. The Courier had been there, and he knew what it was like to see and hear gunfire for the first time. "I'm scared."

"I know, sweetheart, I know. I'll get you out of here, I promise."

The Courier took a trolley from the side of the warehouse and hoisted Iris' barrel onto it, then wheeled her onto the lorry at the door of the warehouse. He made sure to take the other nine barrels so that everything looked official.

To the security guard and the records in the warehouse, he was only a driver doing his job with dedication through the night. To the onlooker, there was nothing suspicious and nothing to question.

After loading the lorry, he drove off, turning left, right and looping back on himself at times, checking if he was being followed. It was clear that he was much more thorough than Annyagh. The Courier had been in worse and more dangerous situations than the one he'd found himself in that evening while driving a teenage girl around in a van.

When he was happy that no one was following him, he pulled over to the side of the road and hopped into the back of the lorry. The Courier walked up to the barrel Iris was in and popped it open.

Iris was huddled in the bottom of the barrel shivering and looking up at him like a rabbit that had been chased down by a fox, wide eyed and terrified.

She rubbed her eyes. "Who are you?"

"A friend."

"What's your name?"

The Courier knew he was to keep his anonymity, so he gave her the only name he knew to use. "Kyle," The Courier said. "I know you're Iris."

"How can I trust you, Kyle?"

"Do you think Jade and Annyagh took you to that warehouse without having a plan? Why do you think they hammered air holes into the barrel? It wasn't just to allow air in, it was a label for me to find you."

She was silent for a short time, studying Kyle intensely.

"You can't trust me fully but I'm your only option and, once you get to know me, you will trust me. I promise."

After a few seconds, Iris stood up and Kyle helped her out of the barrel.

Kyle pulled the shutter down on the back of the van and the pair of them hopped into the cab. Iris clicked in her seatbelt, unable to hide her worry at the next face she was now to entrust her life to.

Kyle turned on the ignition and drove off into the night. The road opened up before these unfamiliar travellers as they carved their way through the countryside to a new destination.

The streetlights guided the way, leading them away from chaos and into something that would hopefully resemble peace.

CHAPTER 28

Iris and Kyle travelled through the night. Right the way up through England and across the border into Scotland. The roads were clear, and the dull hum of the engine was something of a lullaby for Iris as she caught up on the many hours' sleep she'd missed out on the past few days.

At times, she would stir and moan in her sleep. Kyle just stroked her hair and shushed her back to sleep. "Poor wee lassie," he said to himself as she muttered in her dreams.

Kyle wasn't able to place much of what she was saying. At times, he could make out the words 'Jade' and that she was 'scared'. It was clear that she was reliving the events she had experienced that day but at least she wasn't dependent on the medications Dr Rosen was prescribing her in the safehouse.

Looking on, Kyle just hoped that she would be able to handle at least some of what she'd been through herself and Raymond would be able to organise any help for her once they were safely on the Estate.

Bowmore Estate was Raymond's family estate that had been passed down to him from his parents and was in a remote area north of Crieff, towards the Cairngorms.

Kyle lived on the Estate when not placed in locations connected to projects that were linked to business interests of Raymond Campbell or having to watch over the extraction of a young girl from a medical research institution in England.

As I watched over Iris, sleeping on the seat next to Kyle, I knew she would be safe. The man was dedicated to his employer, Raymond, and would do all in his power to protect Iris while she was in his care.

Kyle had a real sense of honour and dedication about him. He was a man who would never turn on someone he cared about and this pride in carrying out his duty was paramount to him.

As Kyle and Iris reached Glasgow, the Sun rose out from behind the tall buildings and air purifiers that dotted the city skyline. The gradually brightening light stirred Iris and she woke. "Where are we?"

"In God's own country," Kyle replied in his Scottish accent with a smile as he glanced a warm look towards Iris. Iris looked blankly at Kyle, totally unaware of who God was and what country he would be from, never mind if he owned one or not. Kyle cleared his throat and removed his smile, knowing that his attempt at humour had failed miserably. "Scotland, Iris. We're in Scotland."

"How long was I sleeping?"

"You slept well, pet. It's only just turned six o'clock. You've had a rough time, darling. Sleep on and I'll wake you when we reach the Estate."

Iris yawned deeply and looked out the window at the city before her. "What is 'the Estate'?" she asked.

Kyle tried to think of a way to explain what 'the Estate' was to a girl who had little experience of the outside world, let alone remote Scotland. "A safe place."

Iris paused, thinking about all that she had been told about the many 'safe' houses and 'safe' places already. "How safe?"

Kyle looked across at the teenage girl staring at him for more than just an answer. Iris wanted reassurance, promises that she wouldn't have to run again. "I will be with you every day, as will Raymond."

"Who is Raymond?"

Kyle didn't want to give too much away about his mysterious employer. "He is the man who owns the Estate and the houses you have been staying in when with Jade and Dr Rosen."

"Is he rich?"

"You could say that," Kyle answered then tried to switch the subject. "He has a few houses on the Estate. The main house is his, but he has a smaller house that I live in. Then, at the back of the Estate, there is a little cottage that his housekeeper used to live in. That is where you will stay."

Iris looked surprised. "I'll have my own house?"

"Well, kind of but not exactly. You won't have to cook anything or look after yourself, that will be my job and the other staff at the house. You will really just use the cottage to eat and sleep in."

"Am I still not allowed to be seen?"

"No, definitely not. Raymond chose the cottage because it is hidden by trees and is right beside my house, so no one will see you and, if you need me, I'm right next door."

"So, it's *your* job to protect me now," Iris asked, desperately trying to clarify roles.

"Yes, that's my job, Iris." Kyle smiled and turned to look at the girl beside him whose eyes reflected the light from the still-rising Sun as they made their way through the city.

Iris nodded in acknowledgement of what Kyle had told her. She was unsure what to make of him and his attempts to make her laugh, but she was sure she would warm to him. There was an inner warmth to Kyle that was palpable, and Iris knew that. Once the trust came and the relationship grew, Iris knew she could trust him with her life and even possibly laugh at some of his jokes.

The miles gradually decreased, and Iris drifted in and out of sleep, Kyle did what he could to make her comfortable. He gave her his coat to use as a blanket or a pillow when she was resting, he stopped for food or drinks when she asked for it and did what he could to make Iris warm to him by telling her awful jokes that made Iris laugh but cringe at the same time.

As Kyle drove north of Crieff and towards the Cairngorms, the mountains rose up and out of the horizon, like prehistoric monoliths, over all they surveyed.

"It's so beautiful," Iris exclaimed, drinking in the scenery with her eyes.

"Like I said, God's own country, pet," Kyle replied, smiling at the girl's reaction to the breathtaking scenery that was stretched out before her, like a constantly scrolling masterpiece that never seemed to end.

Kyle pulled into a gated lane on his left and got out to scan his iris in the access panel on the wall. "Welcome home, Kyle," a female computer voice greeted him as the gate opened slowly ahead of them.

"That screen knows your name," asked Iris, bemused.

"Yes, Iris. Her name is Alana."

"Alana? But is she not a computer?"

"She is, but Raymond spent a lot of money to make sure she sounded welcoming and that was what the computer people came up with. A Logical Automated Neural Assistant – ALANA."

"Hmm," replied Iris, not knowing how to reply to Alana and the sound of the voice she had just heard.

Kyle laughed and shook his head. "He's got more money than sense, pet. I shake my head and laugh every time I drive in here but, when you've got as much money Raymond has, you can have Alana."

Iris laughed, relieved that she wasn't the only

person to find it the whole situation strange. Iris wasn't someone to be rude or insensitive to other people's feelings. She just had a nervous laugh when she didn't know what to make of something or a situation. "I suppose I still don't quite understand the outside world just yet."

Seeing an opportunity to make Iris warm to him more, Kyle replied, "Listen, darlin', I haven't been locked away in a box all my life and I've seen some strange things in my life, but I still can't understand that Alana gizmo."

Iris laughed, and Kyle smiled, finally feeling he was helping this girl to relax and also to see that he may have looked tough on the outside but, on the inside, he was a warm, gentle man who would keep her safe.

Kyle pulled up in front of the main house on Bowmore Estate. The large red-bricked house stood proudly over a large gravel drive and a round fountain with a marble statue pouring water from a jug that was held in the arms of a beautiful young woman.

Large white steps led up to an impressive dark brown double door at the front of the house. All across the front of the house were a series of white wooden-framed windows with smaller square glass panes.

Across the red brick there was a lattice of ivy that was slowly but surely creeping across the front of the house and would gradually cover the whole front if not kept cut back by Raymond's groundskeepers.

The house was beautiful, and Iris stood open-mouthed as she took it all in. "Do you like it then, pet?" Kyle asked, smiling.

"I… I don't know. It's huge."

"I know. Too big for Raymond but he loves it here." Kyle nodded to the view from the main house. The mountains stretched out in front of the Estate, like a scene painted by Claude Monet himself.

"It's beautiful, isn't it?" a voice called from behind them.

Iris turned around to see a tall, slim man with narrow pointed features and round glasses. He wore a blue V-neck jumper and light grey trousers. His dark brown hair was brushed into a side shade and he smiled from ear to ear as he approached her and Kyle from the large, wooden doors.

"I don't know what to say. I…"

"Don't say anything," Raymond replied in his cultured English accent. "Allow me to introduce myself. My name is Raymond Campbell. Welcome to

Bowmore Estate.

"I know your short life outside of The Institute has been nothing short of hellish, but Kyle and I are here to protect you, Iris.

"You are an extraordinary young lady and together we can change this country and this world for the better. Allow us to show you and, you have my word, you will have your freedom."

Raymond held out his hand and Iris shook it tentatively.

Raymond smiled, still holding onto Iris' hand. "You are the future, Iris. You hold this entire world in the palm of that fragile, little hand of yours. Now, let's shape it together."

CHAPTER 29

The Sun was setting in the distance, but it was still warm. The customers, still sitting on their seats outside enjoying the warmth of the summer's evening. A young family sat in the corner of the café, their daughter playing with her doll.

A waitress came towards the table and knelt beside her. "That's a beautiful doll. What's her name?"

The little girl turned and looked into the waitress' eyes. "Poppy."

"Poppy? That's a beautiful name!" the waitress replied. "I love her dress, she really suits red." The waitress stroked the red dress of the little girl's doll before walking back to the counter with her tray.

The little girl looked across at an older man in his fifties, reading a newspaper and drinking a black coffee. Across from him, a girl was sitting reading

Frankenstein by Mary Shelley. She was about fifteen years old, slim, with pale skin and dark auburn hair.

The girl stroked her long, auburn hair behind her ear to sip from the straw of her drink on the table. The girl glanced up to catch the attention of the little girl opposite her, her eyes sparkling in the light.

"You're pretty," the little girl said as she stroked her doll's hair.

"Aw, thank you. So are you! I wish I had blonde hair like yours." The girl's mother laughed politely, and the mother stroked her daughter's hair.

"She's always talking to people," her mother said. "Everywhere we go she likes to make friends."

The man sipped on his coffee and paid close attention to the mother and the little girl. He didn't mean to look suspiciously at the pair, he was just protective of the young girl in his care.

"I'm sure she has lots of friends."

"Too many," the mother replied, "we'll hear all about you in the car on the way home."

"Well you have one more friend today," the older said to the little girl, who was now staring at her.

"Your eyes are so pretty," she said. "I wish I had silver eyes."

The older girl smiled and slid her sunglasses down from the top of her head as she closed her book.

The older man stood up and folded up his newspaper. "I think we'd better go, pet. Your mother will be wondering where we are." The pair stood up calmly and gathered up their things. "My wife's always so obsessive about roast beef night," he said to the young girl's mother in his Scottish accent. "It'll be as tough as old boots but we'll just smile as we eat it, won't we darlin'?"

The older girl smiled and nodded, her long auburn hair tracing lines across her shoulders as her head bobbed.

"It was lovely to meet you, sweetheart," the man said to the little girl with the doll.

"It was nice to meet you too," replied the mother. "Your daughter is beautiful."

"Thank you," the older man replied as he and his daughter strode off into the high street.

As the pair walked, hand in hand, cutting through the shoppers, commuters and tourists, the words rang out in the teenage girl's mind, *'Your eyes are so pretty.'*

The tall, beautiful, auburn-haired girl zipped up her jacket and whispered under her breath, "If only you knew."

ABOUT THE AUTHOR

Scott is an author of young adult fiction from County Down, Northern Ireland, who has worked as a teacher for the past ten years. He is a father of two young children and a sports enthusiast.

His interest in storytelling has been a passion for many years and he is currently working on the Inside

Iris trilogy, as well as short stories and flash fiction.

Scott has written plays and has a keen interest in film, music and drama, which he uses to inspire and shape the fiction he creates in his books.

Scott's first book, *Inside Iris*, is available to download as an eBook and print to order from Amazon. Look out for news of the release date for the second installment of the Inside Iris trilogy.

Connect to Scott via twitter (@SGFiction) and on Instagram (SGFiction) for free content, giveaways and news of upcoming releases and appearances.

For bookings and formal enquiries, Scott can be contacted by email on sgfiction@hotmail.com.

29503896R00172

Printed in Poland
by Amazon Fulfillment
Poland Sp. z o.o., Wrocław